EXCITEMENT, SUSPENSE—AND KAY TRACEY—GO TOGETHER!

Sixteen-year-old Kay Tracey is an amateur detective with a sense of sleuthing that a professional might envy. Her closest friends who share her adventures are Betty Worth and her twin sister Wendy. Whenever there is a mystery in the small town of Brantwood, you'll find Kay and her two friends in the middle of it.

If you like spine-tingling action and heart-stopping suspense, follow the trail of Kay and her friends in the other books in this series: *The Double Disguise, In the Sunken Garden, The Six Fingered Glove Mystery, The Mansion of Secrets,* and *The Message in the Sand Dunes.*

A Kay Tracey Mystery

THE GREEN CAMEO MYSTERY

Frances K. Judd

A BANTAM SKYLARK BOOK

THE GREEN CAMEO MYSTERY

A Bantam Skylark Book/published by arrangement with Lamplight Publishing, Inc.

PRINTING HISTORY

Hardcover edition published in 1978 exclusively by Lamplight Publishing, Inc.
Bantam Skylark edition/October 1980

ISBN 0-553-15071-5

Published simultaneously in the United States and Canada

PRINTED IN THE UNITED STATES OF AMERICA

0 9 8 7 6 5 4 3 2 1

BOOK DESIGNED BY MIERRE

Contents

THE GREEN CAMEO
MYSTERY

Suddenly Kay made up her mind. She would
attempt the swim!

I

The Cameo Curse

"Can I believe my ears?" Kay asked in mock wonder, her brown eyes sparkling.

"Yes, you can," replied blond, vivacious Betty Worth, flourishing a ten-dollar bill. "Here's proof that lunch is my treat today."

"I'll accept with pleasure." Kay laughed. "But what's the special occasion?"

"The money's a reward," explained Betty's twin, serious, dark-haired Wendy. "Mother gave each of us ten dollars for taking care of the house while she was in California."

The girls were just leaving Bartlett's Restaurant on their way to a Saturday afternoon auction.

"Did you enjoy your lunch?" the cashier asked, smiling, as Betty handed her the bill.

"We certainly did——" Kay began, but broke off when she noticed the woman's friendly expression vanish. The cashier was staring intently at the money.

"I'm sorry," she said, "but this is a counterfeit!"

Dead silence followed this startling announcement, until Betty cried:

"Oh, no! How can you tell?"

"I used to work in a bank," the woman replied. "This bill doesn't feel just right. And I'm sure it's a counterfeit we've been warned about." She opened her desk drawer and took out a pamphlet listing current counterfeits.

"This proves it," she said, comparing Betty's money with a genuine ten-dollar bill. "See this picture of a car on the back? The one on the phony money is very blurry."

In a panic Wendy pulled out the bill Mrs. Worth had given her. It too was a counterfeit!

"Mother got these in San Francisco," said Wendy.

"Maybe they're being circulated on the West Coast," Kay speculated.

The cashier advised the girls to notify the Secret Service of the fake money and where it was picked up. Kay paid the check and the three friends hurried to the Tracey car.

"Some treat that turned out to be!" Betty said unhappily, as Kay steered skillfully through heavy traffic.

"Never mind, Betty," she replied. "We'll have fun studying up on counterfeits."

"I know you." Betty winked at Kay. "You won't be happy until you've caught a counterfeiter or two."

"Don't forget, Kay," Wendy added, "right now we're going to an auction. Didn't you say you're bidding on a Chinese desk?"

"Yes." Kay smiled. "My cousin Bill wants it to decorate his new office."

Bill Tracey was a young lawyer who had lived with Kay and her widowed mother for several years.

"I wonder if you'll have much competition in the bidding," said Wendy, who loved old and exotic furniture.

Kay didn't answer. Instead she gasped, and said:

"I nearly forgot. I'm supposed to leave Bill's dress shirt at Sun Sen's laundry. He's going to make a speech soon and needs it."

Turning a corner, Kay drove quickly down the street and pulled up in front of a small hand laundry.

"I'll just be a minute," she said.

Taking a package from the backseat, Kay hopped out and hurried into the little shop. To her surprise, old Sun Sen was not there. Instead, a lovely Chinese woman stood behind the counter.

Wondering who she was, Kay put the package down and smiled. The woman spoke softly with a delightful accent.

"My name Mrs. Wong, and I help my brother who have bad pain. He do work soon as he can rise from couch." She pointed to the rear room of the shop.

Kay said she was sorry to hear that the kind man was ill. She had known and liked him since childhood.

"Has he seen a doctor?" she asked.

To Kay's surprise, a look of fear crossed Mrs. Wong's delicate features.

"No doctor have power against curse of *green cameo*," she said with a slight shiver.

Before Kay could ask what she meant by this strange remark, the phone rang. Murmuring an excuse, the woman lifted the receiver.

"This Lily Wong," she said.

Whatever the Chinese woman heard caused her to turn deathly pale. "No! No!" she gasped.

Kay rushed to Mrs. Wong's side as the woman swayed and dropped the receiver. Then the girl helped her into a chair.

"Cara Noma say green cameo curse strike again," Mrs. Wong sobbed. "Now it hurt my precious Lotus."

Amazed, Kay spoke into the phone, but no one was on the line, so she hung up, and turned back to Mrs. Wong.

"Can you tell me what the trouble is?" she asked gently. Kay really wanted to help the distressed woman, but she was also curious about Mrs. Wong's reference to a mysterious curse.

Between the woman's sobs, Kay slowly drew the story from her. Mrs. Wong had just learned that her daughter, Lotus, was missing from the college she went to.

"I know it is green cameo curse," she moaned. "My husband get it in Shanghai. It bring bad luck to Wongs every three year."

"You mean," Kay asked, astonished, "that a piece of jewelry has brought misfortune to your family every three years?"

Mrs. Wong nodded, and continued in a somber tone, "Yes. Wise men in China tell my husband not buy cameo. But he laugh. Now it is number three day of month. Also year for green cameo to strike! Even Cara Noma cannot break curse!"

"Who is this Cara Noma?" Kay asked.

"She is medium, who can see into future and look back into past. I pay her much money to fight evil curse."

Kay thought, "I'm sure this medium is a fraud, taking advantage of Mrs. Wong."

She asked for more details about Lotus's disappearance, suggesting that maybe she would turn up soon.

"No, no. Cara Noma say my Lotus sell precious jewel box for money to go away."

"How did Cara Noma know this?"

"She live in Lincoln where Lotus go to college."

Lincoln! This was the town where Kay was going to the auction. Her interest awakened, she said:

"Maybe I can find out from Lotus's friends where she is," and explained about her trip to the auction. "My name is Kay Tracey and I've been lucky enough to solve a few mysteries."

Mrs. Wong brightened. "You are most kind," she responded gratefully.

Kay asked the woman if she had a picture of Lotus.

"Yes," she replied and drew a small photograph from her pocket. As she handed it to her, Mrs. Wong said proudly, "Is my flower not lovely?"

Kay nodded in agreement. Indeed Lotus was striking, her sweet, oval face framed by softly combed jet-black hair.

"Take picture of little bride," Mrs. Wong said fondly.

"Bride?" Kay repeated in astonishment.

Lotus's mother said Mr. Wong had arranged a marriage between his daughter and a businessman named Foochow. He was much older than Lotus, but very wealthy.

"Does your daughter love him?" Kay asked.

Mrs. Wong smiled wanly. "We are traditional Chinese, bride have no choice."

Kay was sure that here was a reason for Lotus's disappearance! The girl must have become familiar with American customs while at college, and had decided to run away rather than marry someone she did not know or love. Kay decided not to say this to Mrs. Wong, however. Instead, she assured the woman she would start at once to try to locate the missing girl.

"I've got to go now," Kay said. "I'll let you know as soon as I have any news of Lotus."

The pretty Chinese woman asked Kay to come to her home if she obtained any clue, no matter how slight. She said the address was Lotus Gardens and gave Kay directions for reaching the place.

Kay was surprised by the name. She had seen it at the entrance of a large estate outside Brantwood, where she lived. The place had been sold recently.

"So Mr. Wong is the new owner," she thought. "He must be wealthy to afford such luxury. And his brother-in-law is a poor laundryman!"

Just then Mrs. Wong exclaimed, "Oh, I give you ticket for laundry."

She rose and reached under the counter. An instant later she drew back her hand, crying out. Kay saw that Mrs. Wong had cut her finger, for it was bleeding profusely.

"Will curse of green cameo never end?" Mrs. Wong almost wept, as she clutched her injured finger.

Before Kay could move to help her, the door was flung open, and a tall, pale woman, dressed entirely in black, entered the laundry. She strode swiftly over to Mrs. Wong, who held up her hand and said in a weak voice,

"Cara Noma! Cameo curse again!"

"I will dismiss it at once. Concentrate with me," intoned the medium. To Kay's disgust, Cara Noma started waving her hands above Mrs. Wong's head.

"You know all that hocus-pocus won't do any good," Kay broke in impatiently. "Why don't you bandage Mrs. Wong's finger?" She pulled out a handkerchief.

Cara Noma turned and glared at Kay.

"Child!" she cried harshly. "How dare you interfere?"

"Miss Tracey is good friend," interrupted Mrs. Wong timidly. "She offer to find my Lotus."

"So! Kay Tracey. I've heard of you. Amateur detective. I'm not impressed!" She turned toward Mrs. Wong. "Mrs. Wong, I've warned you not to talk with strangers. I alone can break the curse of the green cameo, and find your daughter!" Mrs. Wong shrank back.

"Some friend you are," Kay said sharply. "Taking this woman's money and telling her a lot of nonsense!"

"Yes," Mrs. Wong said reproachfully, "I give you much money but you do not break curse. Now it come again. My treasure. My Lotus——"

"I need time!" the medium almost shouted. "You must be patient!"

"Oh, leave her alone." Kay's voice was angry. "Mrs. Wong has suffered enough. You're doing her more harm than good!"

Beside herself with fury, Cara Noma lunged at Kay and gripped her arm.

"I will break this curse!" she muttered.

With her other hand, she snatched Mrs. Wong's bleeding finger. Before the astonished girl could free herself, Cara Noma had rubbed a ragged red "X" on Kay's forehead.

"Kay Tracey," she said, an evil look in her eyes, "no one can sneer at my power.

"I transfer the green cameo curse from the house of Wong to *you!*"

II

A Secret Drawer

For a moment Kay was too stunned to utter a word. The medium released her grip on Kay, and darted from Sun Sen's laundry.

In the doorway, she collided with Betty and Wendy. They had gotten worried about their friend's long absence and had decided to find out what was delaying her.

"Watch where you're going!" Cara Noma snapped.

"Sorry," Betty said evenly, "but you might do the same."

The medium's eyes gleamed balefully. "Beware how you speak to me!" she cried shrilly, "or I'll place a curse upon you!"

Betty and Wendy stared. Was the woman crazy? Cara Noma hurried away and disappeared down an alley.

"What a strange woman," Wendy murmured, as they entered the shop. "Positively weird."

"Kay, what have you been doing?" Betty called. "Washing your cousin's shirt?" Then suddenly she saw the bloody mark on her friend's forehead, and gasped:

"Kay! You're hurt!"

"It's not a cut," Kay assured them. She took out a handkerchief and wiped away the stain. "There—see, I'm all right. Cara Noma—that woman you just bumped into—pretended to put the curse of the green cameo on me."

"What in the world is that?" Betty asked.

Kay told the story of the cameo and of Lotus's disappearance. By this time Mrs. Wong returned from the back room where she had gone to wash her cut hand. She smiled warmly at the twins as Kay introduced them.

"Betty and Wendy always help me in solving mysteries," she explained.

"Lily Wong pleased you help her."

"I'm sure the cameo has nothing to do with Lotus's disappearance," Kay said with conviction, "in spite of what Cara Noma tells you. She doesn't have any power. Please forget her and don't worry."

"I will try."

Kay suddenly remembered the missing jewel box, and asked Mrs. Wong to describe it.

"It very beautiful carved chest," she replied. "Made of teakwood. Inlay with rare pearl shell. On cover a green cameo, in shape of lotus blossom."

With a sigh, Mrs. Wong added softly, "Chest betrothal gift to my flower from father."

After assuring Mrs. Wong that they would contact her immediately if they discovered any clue of Lotus, the girls left the shop.

"We'll really have to hurry to reach that auction in time," Kay said, when they were in the car again. "But first I want you to look at this." She showed them the photograph of Lotus Wong.

"Oh!" breathed Wendy admiringly. "She's beautiful."

"Lotus looks like a Chinese princess in that headdress," Betty declared, as she studied the picture.

"She does," Kay agreed. "She's so striking I'm sure we'd recognize her anywhere."

"What do you think could have happened to her?" asked Wendy, as Kay started the car and drove toward Lincoln.

"That's what I intend to find out," Kay replied. "I'm sure, though, that Lotus didn't leave college because of any cameo curse!"

She told them of the girl's engagement to Mr. Foochow.

"I really can't blame her for not wanting to marry a man she's never even met," Wendy said sympathetically.

"I can't either," Betty added. "I think you're right, Kay—that's probably why she left school."

The girls became so engrossed in their discussion of the Wongs and the mystery surrounding them, that they arrived in front of the warehouse in Lincoln almost before they knew it. The sign read:

ANTIQUE FURNITURE BOUGHT AND SOLD

"We're just in time," said Kay as they hurried into the building. "The bidding should begin any minute."

But the start of the auction was delayed, so they had a chance to look around the large room where the sale was to be held.

"Do you see the oriental desk your cousin wants, Kay?" Betty asked, her eyes taking in the various pieces of furniture on display.

Kay finally spotted it across the room and they walked over.

"This is the one, all right!" she exclaimed. "Isn't it a beauty?"

It was a striking and unusual piece, of handsomely carved teakwood.

"It's so exotic!" Wendy commented. "And think, this was all carved by hand!" She ran her fingers lightly over the intricate design on the doors above the writing compartment.

Suddenly Betty nudged Kay. "Oh-oh, there's Mrs. Brindell. She has her eye on the desk, too."

Kay turned to see the wealthy woman she knew well, appraising the desk shrewdly.

"It's a genuine oriental piece," she remarked to a companion. "I'd love to own it."

After Mrs. Brindell and her friend walked away, the girls looked through the interior of the desk. They were intrigued by the many cubbyholes and drawers.

"What's this, I wonder?" Kay said, as she pushed a tiny sliding panel. She was startled by a sharp *click*.

A hidden drawer flew open!

"Perfect hiding place for money." Kay laughed.

On an impulse she dropped the envelope containing Bill's hundred dollars into the secret compartment and closed it. Betty laughed. In a deep voice she said:

"I place the curse of the green cameo on this drawer! Never shall it open again!"

Kay scarcely heard her, for an object on a table next to the desk caught her eye. It was a teakwood jewel case. Every detail of it fitted the one Mrs. Wong had described as belonging to her daughter!

Kay looked once more, hardly daring to believe what she saw. Yes—it must be the same chest because on the lid was a green cameo, with the design of a lotus flower.

"Betty! Wendy!" she whispered tensely. "Look!"

The twins followed her gaze, and could scarcely keep from crying aloud as they, too, recognized the jewel case.

"I wish I could bid on it," Kay said. "I'm sure Mrs. Wong would want to keep the chest in the family."

"I can lend you ten dollars," Betty offered. "A good bill this time."

"I have five," Wendy counted.

"And I have ten," added Kay, as she quickly opened the secret compartment again, took out the envelope and slipped it into her purse.

"Well, imagine seeing you here!" a voice rasped near them.

Kay and the twins whirled to face Chris Eaton, a disagreeable schoolmate who liked to play under-handed tricks on Kay and her friends.

"Hello," Kay said. "Are you bidding today?"

"Yes, and you may as well save your breath—and your pennies—if you have any," Chris went on contemptuously, "for I have plenty to bid on that jewel case you've been eyeing."

She flashed a wad of money before them. Although Kay and the twins ignored Chris's remarks, they hoped anxiously that their enemy would not be able to outbid Kay for the carved chest.

"Ladeez and gents." The auctioneer's booming voice aroused the bidders to alert attention. "Please be seated."

Quickly the girls took seats. The man indicated the Chinese desk with a sweeping gesture.

"This here's a genu-wine hand-carved piece, made in China, and it's to be auctioned together with that bee-yu-ti-ful jewel box you see next to it."

Kay gasped! The two were to be sold as a set. Her heart thumped wildly. She might have a chance at both the desk and the carved chest, if the bidding did not go too high!

Betty and Wendy whispered encouragement as the auctioneer lifted his gavel to start the bidding. Chris Eaton cleared her throat importantly. With a sly glance at Kay, she smiled smugly.

"In view of the value of these pieces," the auctioneer announced, "no bid under $125 will be considered."

Down crashed the gavel, and with it, Kay's hopes. The twins glanced at her in quick sympathy. The sum was all the money Kay and the twins had with them!

The first bid was $130. Mrs. Brindell quickly jumped it to $150. Then an elderly gentleman said $160. Suddenly the girls realized that Chris had not joined in the bidding. Kay glanced her way and Chris's sullen face was a study in bafflement and anger that made Kay laugh. Evidently Chris did not have enough money either!

"She sure put that bankroll away in a hurry," Betty remarked with a smile.

Though unable to bid, Kay turned her attention to the auctioneer. He was boosting a heated contest between Mrs. Brindell and the elderly man.

"Do I hear two-sixty?" the auctioneer chanted.

The wealthy woman shrugged and shook her head, apparently refusing to bid higher.

"I'll give two fifty-seven," called out her competitor.

There was a complete silence. The auctioneer

looked around, and once more raised the mallet.

"I have two fifty-seven! Two fifty-seven! Do I hear two-sixty?" He paused, hopeful Mrs. Brindell would speak up. But she kept still.

"Going for two fifty-seven—going——" The wooden gavel swung downward.

Before the auctioneer could complete the sale, there was a sudden commotion, and a man rushed forward.

"Wait! Wait!" he shouted commandingly. "You can't sell the desk! It's mine!"

III

A Costly Mistake

The crowd at the auction was thrown into an uproar as the stranger elbowed his way forward.

"What do you mean—this desk belongs to you?" demanded the auctioneer.

"My name's Sidney Trexler," he announced pompously. "I stored this desk here some time ago."

"Well, you must owe a lot on back charges," replied the auctioneer, glaring at the man. "You know our rule. After six months we have a right to——"

"I know, I know," Trexler broke in rudely. "I'm going to settle the payments. Here." He held out several bills.

The auctioneer frowned. "The desk has already been sold to the highest bidder," he said doubtfully. "It's up to him."

Trexler raised his voice belligerently. "I've got a right to my own property. I'm getting married soon and I need it!"

At this point the man who had made the highest offer for the Chinese set came forward.

"I don't want any unpleasantness," he addressed Trexler. "If the desk is yours, by all means take it." He turned on his heel and walked away.

The auctioneer shrugged. "Okay, Mr. Trexler, see the manager and pay the charges."

"Right." Trexler smiled in self-satisfaction as he started away. Then suddenly he turned back. Pointing to the cameo chest, he asked, "Since that was going with the desk, maybe I can buy it cheap."

"Nothing doing," interrupted the auctioneer. "I'm putting the chest up again right now. I've got to make some profit around here!"

Kay and the twins had been watching the scene with intense interest, each wondering what would happen to the carved jewel box. Now, at the auctioneer's last words, Kay cried out impulsively:

"How much to start the bidding?"

"Fifty dollars, miss," replied the man, and once more raised the gavel. "Fifty-one. Fifty-one. Do I hear fifty-one?"

A murmur ran through the group. Betty and Wendy looked at Kay questioningly.

"Are you going to bid?" Betty whispered.

"If the case *is* Lotus's, I'm sure Mrs. Wong will buy it back. Fifty-one!" she called out.

"Fifty-five dollars," shrilled Chris Eaton, throwing Kay a defiant glance.

"Oh, that pest's still here," Betty muttered. "Don't give her a chance, Kay!"

But before Kay could bid again, Mrs. Brindell called, "Sixty."

Kay clutched her shoulderbag nervously. The

wealthy woman could easily outbid her.

Nevertheless, Kay raised Mrs. Brindell's offer to sixty-five. For a moment there was silence among the bidders. Kay's pulse hammered rapidly. Was she doing the right thing?

"Sixty-five dollars from the young lady—do I hear seventy?" chanted the auctioneer.

The twins caught their breath, then were dismayed to hear Chris's nasal voice:

"I'll bid seventy-two fifty."

Wendy moaned softly. "She's just doing it for spite!"

"Seventy-two fifty—do I hear more for this gem of the Orient?"

The auctioneer looked directly at Kay.

She took a deep breath. Suppose it wasn't Lotus's chest! Suppose Mrs. Wong wouldn't buy it! Yet something impelled her to go on.

"Seventy-five." Kay decided this would be her limit. She could not risk another cent of Bill's money.

Every eye in the room focused on Kay and Chris.

"Seventy-five," echoed the auctioneer. "Do I hear eighty?"

Kay's pretty face was flushed from the excitement. Would the green cameo chest be hers?

The auctioneer raised his gavel slightly.

"Eighty," came Chris's deliberate drawl.

Kay clenched her hands and fought back a choking sensation. If only Chris knew what the jewel box would mean to Mrs. Wong! Kay felt certain the spiteful girl didn't want it for herself that badly.

"She's just trying to beat me," Kay thought bitterly. "But she's hurting poor Mrs. Wong instead."

"Does it go for eighty?" the auctioneer began his

routine. He was interrupted by a man's voice from the rear of the room.

"I'll bid eighty-five for the case."

Everyone turned to see Sidney Trexler waving his hand for attention. "Eighty-five," he repeated.

The smirk had disappeared from Chris's face. Betty noted this and said aloud:

"Miss Moneybags seems to be out of funds!"

Those standing near laughed, and Chris scowled.

No one raised Trexler's offer, so the auctioneer concluded the sale. The owner of the Chinese desk marched up to claim the jewel box.

Kay, listening closely, overheard Trexler remark to the auctioneer:

"I got a bargain after all."

The girls stood up from their chairs. As they walked toward the door Mrs. Brindell stopped Kay.

"Hello, my dear," she said. "It's too bad you were disappointed in your bid."

"Maybe I'll be luckier next time," the girl replied cheerfully.

"Since you appreciate fine old things," the woman added, "I'd like to take you to another sale sometime."

Kay said she would enjoy that very much, and caught up to the twins.

"My," Betty commented, impressed by Mrs. Brindell's interest in Kay. "You really caught her attention!"

"Yes," Wendy agreed, "but look over there—you've missed something!"

Following her friend's gaze, Kay was astonished to see Chris Eaton talking and laughing with Sidney Trexler.

"Look at that!" exclaimed Wendy, her eyes wide. "They're leaving together!"

Indeed, Trexler and Chris were leaving the auction room together.

The three girls reached the sidewalk in time to see them enter a restaurant across the street.

"Well!" Betty declared in disgust. "Wouldn't you think even Chris would be smarter than that? Didn't she hear Mr. Trexler say he's getting married?"

"I suppose she thinks she's being real clever!" was Wendy's scornful comment.

Kay reserved her opinions on Chris's actions. Maybe she was going to buy the jewel box from him.

After dropping the twins off at their home, she continued on her way to Bill's office.

"Well, did you get it?" he asked eagerly, as Kay dropped into a chair opposite him.

She shook her head unhappily. "No—I couldn't even begin to bid on it," Kay sighed. "The bidding started at a hundred and twenty-five. Then the owner showed up at the last minute and claimed it. So even a thousand dollars wouldn't have helped."

Kay gave a vivid account of the auction sale, and was just about to relate the incident of the cameo chest when she remembered that Bill's money was still in her bag. She took out the envelope and opened it.

"Why—oh——" she cried out.

"What is it, Kay?"

"Your money! It's gone!" Kay frantically emptied the contents of her bag on the lawyer's desk but there was no sign of the money.

"Perhaps it slipped out of your purse into the car," Bill suggested.

"No, no!" Kay was nearly in tears. "This envelope. It isn't mine!"

"What do you mean?"

"I tossed your envelope into a secret drawer in that

Chinese desk!" Kay groaned. "I must have pulled out another one. Yours is still in the desk!" Kay picked up the phone book.

"I'm going to call the warehouse. Oh, I hope Mr. Trexler hasn't taken the desk away!"

There was no answer at the Lincoln building, however. It was past closing time but Kay refused to give up hope.

"I'll call there first thing on Monday," she said. "But right now I'll retrace my route. Maybe I'll see Mr. Trexler."

As she ran from the office, Kay suddenly thought of the curse that Cara Noma had pronounced on her. It seemed to be working!

She was about to open the car door, when she was greeted by a mocking voice. "Hello Kay. You don't look very happy. Too much auction?"

Kay was annoyed to see Chris Eaton looking at her slyly, and decided not to say anything about her problems.

"Not at all," she replied casually. But Kay could not resist adding, "You weren't so fortunate yourself."

"Wasn't I though!" Chris contradicted. "I had a delightful talk with Mr. Trexler. He treated me to a soda. Said it was to make up for outbidding me."

"I wouldn't be too overwhelmed," Kay said flatly.

"You're just jealous you weren't invited!" Chris snapped. "Anyhow, he told me all about wanting that cameo box for his fiancée."

Kay was surprised that Trexler had confided so much to Chris, but did not wish to encourage her with any questions. She was about to break away, when Chris announced dramatically:

"And do you know what else? Mr. Trexler said his

fiancée's a beautiful Chinese princess. He met her at college!"

"A—Chinese princess?" Kay echoed. Then she asked quickly, "What's her name?"

"Well—he didn't say," Chris admitted. "But he did show me her photograph."

Was Lotus Wong Trexler's fiancée? Was he the reason the Chinese girl had fled from school? Impulsively Kay took Lotus's picture from her bag.

"Is this Mr. Trexler's fiancée?" she inquired tensely. Chris glanced at the picture and answered without hesitation, "Yes! Where'd you get this?"

"That's all I want to know!" Kay exclaimed, without answering Chris's question.

In another moment she was in the car and on her way to Sun Sen's laundry.

IV

Detecting A Fake

———————◆———————

Kay burst into Sun Sen's laundry. The front of the shop was empty, and she was afraid for a moment that Mrs. Wong had already left. But she heard light footsteps and the pretty woman came from the back.

At the sight of Kay, her delicate features lit up in a charming smile. "Miss Tracey! So happy to see you again. But the shirt not ready—my poor brother——"

"Never mind, Mrs. Wong," Kay broke in. "I came back to tell you I may have news of Lotus, and——"

"You know where she is? My flower returns?" The woman's liquid, almond-shaped eyes filled with tears of sudden joy.

"I'm sorry. It's nothing so definite as that," Kay replied. "I've just come from an auction, where I saw a carved box exactly like the one you described as your daughter's."

Mrs. Wong was at first obviously disappointed that Lotus had not been found. But she listened intently as Kay told her about the auction and her meeting with

Chris without mentioning the fact that Lotus might be planning to marry Trexler.

"Did you ever hear of Sidney Trexler?" Kay asked.

"No. He is stranger to me. You say he buy box Lotus sold?"

"Yes, and then," Kay said, "when this—acquaintance of mine saw Lotus's photo, she was positive it was the same girl whose picture Mr. Trexler had shown her."

"So we must see if Mr. Trexler buy cameo box back for Lotus," said Mrs. Wong. "You can find him?" she asked eagerly.

"I think he can be reached through the people at that warehouse," responded Kay assuringly. "It's closed, now, so on Monday I'll ask about him. Then perhaps you and I can go to see him."

"Yes, yes, I meet you whenever you say," agreed Mrs. Wong. She seemed suddenly apprehensive, as if an unpleasant thought had crossed her mind. "I try to be patient—but right now fear of green cameo curse come over me—what Cara Noma call thought wave—that jewel's evil power pursues Lotus."

Kay, to soothe Mrs. Wong's fears, suggested that when Lotus sold the box perhaps she had released herself from the evil influence. The idea seemed to appeal to Mrs. Wong who sighed in relief.

"You very good friend," she said. "Lily——"

She stopped abruptly as a low moan issued from the room in the back. For a moment Kay was frightened. Then, remembering that Sun Sen was lying ill back there, she said, "Mrs. Wong, please let me call a doctor. He'll know best how to help your brother—better than that medium. And please promise not to tell Cara Noma what I've told you."

Mrs. Wong hesitated before replying. "I will say

nothing to Cara Noma," she finally agreed. "Please to call doctor."

Before leaving Kay phoned Doctor Smith, and was assured he would hurry over to take care of Sun Sen. Mrs. Wong accompanied Kay to the door, thanking her profusely.

"You are kind and sweet like my Lotus," she said gratefully.

Impulsively, Kay grasped the woman's dainty hand. "I want to meet your beautiful daughter. Good-bye now until Monday."

As Kay drove home, her mind was spinning. "I must do everything possible to help Mrs. Wong," she thought. "I wonder what her husband is like. She's afraid of him, I'm sure. And that awful Cara Noma—using Mrs. Wong's superstition and worry to make money!"

At supper Kay told Bill apologetically that she had been unable to locate the lost money.

"If I can catch up with the owner of the desk," she said, "he'll have to let me look in that secret compartment. I only hope your money's still there."

"It was very careless of you, Kay," her mother remarked. "Very unlike you, too. You must have had something else on your mind."

"I did," Kay agreed.

For the next few minutes Kay kept her family spellbound with the story of the Wongs' troubles and Cara Noma's part in it.

"It seems like a fairy tale," Mrs. Tracey remarked. "And smearing blood on you, Kay. How awful!"

"Sounds as if that medium actually did rub some bad luck on you, Kay." Bill managed a faint smile.

"I'll get that money back or take a summer job and earn it!" Kay declared.

"Knowing you for the detective you are, I imagine you'll find it in no time. Did you offer to find Lotus?"

"Of course."

"Well, take a tip from me," the young lawyer advised. "Don't become too involved with laundries and Lotus Gardens."

"Be kind but careful," Kay's mother added.

Kay promised, then told them of the counterfeit bills which Mrs. Worth had brought from San Francisco. Fortunately the two she had given the twins were the only fake ones she had.

"I'm going to study up on counterfeits," Kay remarked.

"It's a fascinating subject," replied Bill. "But each new set of phony money has a different flaw, so you can't go entirely by past experience."

Sunday afternoon found Kay and the twins studying the counterfeit bills in Kay's bedroom. On the old maple desk beside them lay an encyclopedia open to the page on counterfeits.

"I feel so official!" exclaimed Betty, as she took the magnifying lens which Kay handed her, "Secret Service Department, here I come!" She peered closely through the glass at the money. "Not so many little red and blue silk fibers in it as a regular ten."

"There's a test you can do without the glass," Kay said.

"Show us," Wendy said excitedly.

"Need any help?" Betty offered.

"No," Kay said. "All you need is a good sense of touch. It's really simple."

Kay picked up one of the ten-dollar bills. The twins watched, fascinated, as she began rubbing it firmly between her thumb and forefinger.

"Sure enough!" she exclaimed, after stroking the

counterfeit for some moments. "The paper remains stiff—doesn't soften up at all."

"I get the idea," Betty said. "If the bill is genuine, and you keep on rubbing it, the money will feel like cloth—linen maybe."

"That's right."

"Who has a real ten? I want to try it," Wendy said, eagerly.

None of them did, but Kay drew some one-dollar bills from her wallet.

The three friends became engrossed in the rubbing test, first with the good bills, then with the counterfeit money.

Suddenly Betty giggled. "If we don't look like a bunch of misers! Stroking these bills as if our lives depended on them!"

"Someone's life *is* depending on making phony bills like these," declared Kay. "We don't have much to go on, but I'd love to find some lead to the origin of this racket."

"Never mind," said Betty. "Once you set your mind to it, you'll turn up a clue."

"Thanks for your faith," Kay responded, laughing. "But the trail to San Francisco is a long one. Meantime, I need your help in a case closer to home—finding Lotus Wong."

"Oh, yes, I'd almost forgotten her—the unhappy bride-to-be," Betty replied gravely.

"For better or worse," Wendy added dreamily.

> *"Oh cruel fate!*
> *How sad a state!*
> *Wounded pride.*
> *A missing bride."*

Betty groaned and added:

> *"Let it ne'er be said*
> *That we twins have fled*
> *From an adventure gay*
> *With our friend Kay——"*

"Oh, no!" Wendy laughed. "Now my sister's composing verses."

"At least they rhyme," commented Kay, "and not bad for the spur of the moment."

Just then Mrs. Tracey called, "Kay, telephone for you, dear."

Her daughter hurried downstairs. Picking up the receiver, she said pleasantly: "Hello——"

For a moment there was no reply. Finally came a voice so faint that Kay could hardly hear it.

"This Lily Wong. Miss Tracey, no meet you Monday. Maybe you come Lotus Gardens Tuesday—in afternoon. I tell you——"

"Yes?" Kay asked, as the woman paused.

The only answer was a *click*. Mrs. Wong had hung up!

V

A Close Escape

Rising apprehension gripped Kay, as she replaced the telephone. Of one thing she was certain. Mrs. Wong had not wanted anyone to overhear her call to Kay.

"She's very afraid of whoever interrupted her call to me," Kay reasoned. "Mr. Wong? Or was it Cara Noma?"

Suddenly she thought of her cousin's warning. Should she go to Lotus Gardens?

"Something wrong, dear?" Mrs. Tracey had entered the hall, and noticed her daughter's perplexed expression. "As if I need to ask," she sighed. "That was Mrs. Wong?"

Kay repeated the conversation, and her mother's brow puckered.

"I won't forbid you to go to Lotus Gardens," she said, "but I'm going with you!"

"Good. Mrs. Wong needs some sympathy," Kay

said, looking fondly at Mrs. Tracey, "and you are just the person to give it to her!"

The Worths came downstairs, saying they had to go home.

"Good night, Mrs. Tracey. See you in the morning, Kay."

Before leaving 'for school next day, Kay made a call to the Lincoln warehouse. She asked if Mr. Trexler's desk and cameo jewel case were still there.

"Why no," replied the man who had answered. "Mr. Trexler took the case with him, and had a truck pick up the desk right after the auction."

Kay's heart sank. "Can you give me the address where the desk was sent?" she asked anxiously.

The man consulted his records, then said, "I'm sorry, miss, there's no shipping point mentioned. Mr. Trexler had a van move the desk."

"Probably to his home. Where is that?"

"I really couldn't say. We haven't his present address."

"Can you tell me the name of the trucking company that moved the desk?" Kay next asked.

"No, I don't know that either, but I heard Mr. Trexler say something about Carmont."

Discouraged, she hung up the phone. "Well," Kay sighed, "it looks as if I'll spend my afternoon chasing around to every trucking company in Carmont."

At lunch she passed the news along to the twins, who said they would help her.

"We brought our car today," said Wendy. "I'll drive you around after school is over."

Their first stop was at a Carmont drugstore, where Kay consulted a telephone directory, and copied the names of all trucking companies and warehouses.

Fifteen minutes later, they pulled up in front of the

first name on the list—a warehouse. Kay went into the office and asked whether they had moved Mr. Trexler's desk. No such shipment had been recorded.

Kay was given the same disappointing answer at one warehouse and trucking company after another. Growing less hopeful by the moment, the girls went to a company on the outskirts of the town. While the twins waited, Kay went inside and repeated her question somewhat mechanically to the woman clerk.

"Yes, Mr. Trexler's desk is here," she was told.

Kay's fatigue vanished instantly. "I'd very much like to see it, if I may," she requested politely.

The woman eyed her suspiciously. "Really, miss—that's against our policy. We absolutely cannot show it to you without Mr. Trexler's permission."

Kay knew this was only to be expected, but tried once more to persuade the woman.

"Oh, please—it's very important, and——"

"Listen, young lady, I don't know you from a hole in the wall."

"Here's my driver's license."

"That makes no difference. Dishonest people have licenses. I can't show you the desk."

Kay was upset, but kept her head. She asked for Trexler's address. This time the woman really became angry.

"You don't even know where he lives and you want to look at his property! You really have a lot of nerve! Good-bye." Kay knew the situation was hopeless.

"Hey, what happened to you?" Betty asked when Kay came out. "You look as if the sun had burned you to a crisp!"

"I'm burned up all right," Kay replied, and told them what had happened.

"Let's get the police," Wendy suggested.

Kay glanced at her watch. "The place will close any second. It's five-thirty now. I'll ask Bill what to do."

As Wendy drove toward Brantwood, Kay asked her to take the road that led past the Wong estate.

"Uh, oh," said Betty, "Wendy will start dreaming of old Chinese pagodas and run us in a ditch for sure."

"Fear not, sister mine," Wendy replied, unperturbed by Betty's teasing. "I'll get us all there in one piece."

A short while later they turned into the narrow, tree-lined road that led to Brantwood, and cruised smoothly along toward Lotus Gardens.

"You know—it's very odd, when you think of it," Betty commented, "Mrs. Wong's brother running a small hand laundry, while she lives in luxury in such a gorgeous place."

"Yes," Kay said, "I think so too. Mr. Wong evidently runs a profitable business—wouldn't you think he'd make life a little easier for poor sick Sun Sen?"

"Maybe Mr. Wong's ashamed to have Sun Sen as a brother-in-law and wants to ignore him," said Wendy.

"I bet Mr. Wong's not very kind to his family. I wonder what Lotus thinks of her father."

"When you go there tomorrow, you'll be able to study the master of Lotus Gardens in his home environment," declared Betty. "Who knows—maybe old Wong spends his time in one of those secret Chinese dens——"

Wendy shivered a little. "Oh, Betty! Your imagination is wilder than mine." She sped up.

"Not so fast, Wendy!" Betty cautioned.

Her sister seemed to be oblivious to the warning.

"*Look out!*" Kay screamed, as their car hurtled toward a crossroad.

Too late, Wendy saw another car shoot out from the left. She jammed on the brake, and swerved wildly. Fortunately, the other car turned sharply just ahead of them, so a serious collision was narrowly missed.

Wendy pulled up to an abrupt stop half off the road. She leaned back, trembling, too weak from fright to say a word.

"That was too close for comfort," was all Betty could manage, and took a deep breath.

Kay said shakily, "It was a narrow miss." Suddenly she sat up straight. "Hey look!"

The car they had missed had stopped about one hundred feet ahead. The driver was glaring in their direction.

"That woman," Kay said tensely, "is Cara Noma! Now we're in for it!"

VI

A Tinkling Trap

―――――――――◆―――――――――

"I don't want that woman wishing any bad luck on me!" cried Wendy.

Instead of getting out of her car and heaping abuse upon Kay and the twins, Cara Noma remained seated. But she began to make strange motions with her hands:

"Look!" Betty said in surprise. "She's going through some sort of ritual!"

Though her face remained stony, Cara Noma fixed the three friends with a piercing gaze.

Wendy shuddered. "Do you think she's putting another curse on us?"

"It's just an act to frighten us into turning back." Kay's tone was scornful. "I bet she's headed for the Wong estate."

"Then let's take another road," begged Wendy. "She's likely to make trouble."

"She wouldn't dare try anything against three of

us," Betty said with assurance. "Go ahead, Wendy."

Her sister managed a faint smile. "Okay, but you drive, Betty. I've had my share of it for the day."

Before Betty could take the wheel, Cara Noma had started away. Minutes later, the girls were riding toward Brantwood again. As Betty swung the car around a bend, Kay exclaimed, "There's the Wong estate!"

"Lotus Gardens," murmured Wendy dreamily. "It's like a magic garden!"

Before them stretched an expanse of velvety-green lawn, splashed with the brilliant colors of exotic flowers.

"Look at that miniature bridge." Kay pointed toward a quaint rustic structure, arching over a tiny brook.

Even the mansion had been given a touch of the Orient with its pagodalike roof, and the place was surrounded by delicate, feathery trees.

On a sudden hunch Kay asked Betty to turn into the long, curving driveway. Seeing Cara Noma's car parked almost out of sight under a clump of trees, she suggested they stop near it.

"Hide our car too," Kay suggested. "I want to do a little sleuthing."

After the car was screened by some bushes, the girls went forward on foot. Hearing voices, they hurried silently along a narrow path at the side of the house. Presently they came to a small garden well hidden by a high, blooming hedge.

Parting the hedge, the twins saw a strange scene. The medium, dressed in her usual somber black, was making peculiar signs and chanting weird-sounding phrases. Mrs. Wong was seated on a stone bench, looking at her as if hypnotized!

"Mrs. Wong's practically in a trance," Kay said in alarm. "It was Cara Noma who kept her from meeting me!"

They were even more astonished when they saw Mrs. Wong reach into her pocket almost mechanically and give a handful of bills to the medium.

"Look at all the money that woman's taking from Mrs. Wong," Betty said, shocked.

"This has gone too far!" Kay said grimly.

She rushed from her hiding place to a break in the hedge, followed by the twins. Catching sight of them, Cara Noma pulled Mrs. Wong from the bench and steered her swiftly out a rear entrance of the garden.

"Mrs. Wong!" Kay called. "Wait! We've come to help you!"

But her words fell on empty air. When the girls reached the opening, there was no sign of Cara Noma or Mrs. Wong.

"They've gone into the house!" Kay said. "We'd better hurry round to the front door."

They rang the bell and the door was opened by a Chinese servant. Kay was struck by his unusual height. He was the tallest Oriental man she had ever seen. As calmly as she could, Kay said, "Please tell Mrs. Wong that Kay Tracey is here."

"Chang will tell his mistress," he replied without any Oriental accent. Then he invited them to come in.

Chang led the way across an immense hall with a highly polished floor to a richly furnished living room. As the servant motioned the girls toward a silk-covered couch, he scrutinized Kay closely. So closely, in fact, that she was a bit uncomfortable.

After he left, Kay remembered her mother's warning. Maybe she had been too hasty in coming here. She was roused from her thoughts by the man's return.

"Mrs. Wong is busy at present," he announced, "and begs that the young ladies make themselves comfortable while they await her."

"But——" Kay began, growing impatient.

"I shall return to serve the ladies tea," the servant interrupted. Bowing slightly, he left the room.

"Looks as if we'll be having a tea party without a hostess," Betty remarked wryly.

"I wouldn't drink their tea," said Wendy in a scared voice. "It might be poisoned!"

"Oh, don't be silly," said Betty.

"This is ridiculous!" Kay exploded. "I'm going to find Mrs. Wong. I'm sure she's still in the clutches of that medium."

"We'll go with you," said Betty. "You'd better not roam around this place by yourself."

"The green cameo may harm you," added Wendy uneasily.

"Oh,—don't tell me you're falling for that stupid superstition too," Kay said and walked determinedly toward the doorway. "You stay here, in case Mrs. Wong shows up while I'm gone."

Waving them back, Kay walked into the hall and out of the twins' sight. She stole along softly, thinking how eerily silent it was. Kay looked into various rooms but saw no one.

"Cara Noma and Mrs. Wong may be upstairs," she thought, "but I'll look down here first."

Suddenly the girl became aware of a faint tinkling sound. It seemed to come from directly ahead. It was then that Kay noticed a massive, carved door at the very end of the hall.

"That bell ringing's probably part of Cara Noma's act," she thought, and walked up to the closed door. She listened closely for a moment.

"Yes," Kay decided, "I can hear it more clearly now."

She placed her hand on the knob, but for the first time was hit with a sense of fear. She glanced quickly over her shoulder, half-expecting to find someone watching her. But the hall was still deserted.

With determination Kay turned the knob, and pushed the door open cautiously. There was one dimly lit lamp in the room, revealing rich oriental hangings that covered all the walls. Apparently there were no windows. No one was in sight.

Across the room Kay saw a string of tiny colored glass bells hanging on an arched stand beside a table. They swayed gently back and forth, creating their own music.

"How odd!" Kay thought, realizing that there was no breeze to cause the movement of the bells.

Then her eyes caught sight of a narrow silk cord attached to the bells. The end of the cord disappeared behind a bamboo screen.

Someone must be behind that screen, pulling the rope that jingled the bells; Kay felt a chill go down her spine, but she asked aloud, "Mrs. Wong, are you in here?"

A soft, sinister chuckle came from back of the screen. Then there was a few moments of silence, as Kay and the unknown bell ringer each waited for the other one to make a move.

Convinced that Cara Noma was the person, Kay tiptoed forward. No doubt she had Mrs. Wong in a trance behind the screen. Kay shivered. She knew that once in a while a medium failed to bring her subject out of a hypnotic state.

As Kay neared the screen, the light suddenly went out. In the pitch blackness a hand reached toward Kay, and slapped her so hard she was stunned. Groggy, she fell into a chair, barely conscious of figures scuttling past her, and a door being opened and closed.

Finally gathering her senses, Kay became aware of a strong sweet fragrance. Turning her head, she noted that on the table before her burned a steady green flame.

"It must be incense," Kay thought, as the light vaguely revealed a burner in the shape of a Chinese god.

Unable to rouse herself, Kay stared in fascination, breathing the pleasant scent deeply. It was so very, very soothing.

Soon Kay felt a delicious, drowsy warmth creep over her. She dropped her head upon the arm of the chair, and fell into a deep sleep.

VII

Under A Spell

Back in the living room of the Wong home, Wendy and Betty Worth fidgeted. Where was Kay? Where was Chang? The servant had never returned with the tea.

"Wendy, we must find Kay!" Betty said at last.

"But where do we start to look in this huge place?" asked Wendy.

But Betty didn't wait for an answer. As she started out of the door, she almost collided with Chang, who was coming in with a large teakwood tray. On it were dainty sandwiches and a tea service.

"Oh!" he said. "You are leaving? I am very sorry to have been so long."

Betty backed into the room, and as the man set the tea service on a small table, she told him that Kay had left them and not returned. Chang's face took on a strange look.

"But did she not wish to see Mrs. Wong?"

The twins did not know how to answer him. If they told him their suspicions of Cara Noma, Kay might be annoyed. And Chang himself behaved oddly. It was possible he was involved with the medium.

"Where is Mrs. Wong?" Betty asked abruptly.

"She is upstairs, but will be down shortly," Chang replied.

Betty looked at him searchingly. A little while before he had told the girls that Mrs. Wong would soon be down to see them. Had he been telling the truth?

Everyone's question was answered by the sudden appearance of Mrs. Wong in the doorway. She looked very pale and not completely steady on her feet. But the pretty little woman seemed to be in full command of her faculties and graciously asked the girls to sit down.

"Your friend go away?" she asked.

Wendy and Betty were almost too flabbergasted to speak, but Betty finally found her voice.

"Why, Mrs. Wong, haven't you seen Kay?"

"No. Will you girls have sugar in tea?" the woman said almost dreamily.

Wendy and Betty looked at each other. What was going on in this strange house?

Chang had already been dismissed by his mistress. In a quiet voice Wendy told Mrs. Wong that Kay, fearing Cara Noma might harm Mrs. Wong, had gone to find the two women.

There was a faraway look in Mrs. Wong's eyes as she asked slowly, "Cara Noma? I have not seen Cara Noma for several days."

"But you were in the garden with her a little while ago——" began Wendy.

"Lily Wong in garden with Cara Noma only in spirit," she replied.

This was too much for the girls. If Mrs. Wong

really believed this, there was no doubt that Cara Noma had terrible control over the woman. They had already seen the medium take money from the unsuspecting woman. No telling what other sinister motives Cara Noma might have.

This thought made the Worth twins more worried about Kay's long absence. Standing up, Betty said that she would like Mrs. Wong's permission to search the house. Something must have gone wrong or Kay would have returned.

Mrs. Wong looked puzzled. "Everything quiet in house. Nothing happen, Lily sure."

Nevertheless, the woman got up and accompanied the two girls into the hall. She invited them to go from room to room with her to find Kay. When they reached the small room in which Kay lay asleep, the small woman sniffed.

"Incense burn in there," she said, a frown creasing her forehead.

Quickly she opened the door and snapped on a light. The woman gasped when she saw Kay slumped in the chair. Betty and Wendy rushed forward and grabbed their friend's arms.

"Kay! Kay! Wake up!" Wendy cried, terrified.

The sudden shaking brought Kay out of her sleep. But she gazed up in bewilderment at those in the room, seemingly unable to comprehend where she was.

"She needs fresh air," cried Betty.

Together the twins helped Kay to the hall, and into a nearby room where the window was open. In a few moments she was fully awake.

She stared at Mrs. Wong.

"Oh yes, now I remember! I was looking for you. Where is Cara Noma?"

Mrs. Wong gave Kay the same answer that she had

given the twins. Obviously she had been in a hypnotic state and knew nothing about Cara Noma's visit to the house. They all walked back to the living room.

The girls thought it was very strange that their hostess did not ask how Kay happened to be in the room and who had lighted the incense burner. She still acted as though she were in a trance, and mechanically poured the tea and offered sandwiches to her guests.

The girls ate hardly anything, saying they were expected home, and must leave at once. Mrs. Wong would not let them go until she had shown them more pictures of her daughter, and again received Kay's promise to try to locate her.

"One question, Mrs. Wong," said Kay. "Does your husband know that Lotus has disappeared?"

Mrs. Wong's dreamy expression changed to a look of fright. She shook her head.

"Husband become angry—like madman. He no learn about Lotus," she whispered tensely.

Kay suggested having the police look for Lotus, but Mrs. Wong waved this suggestion aside.

"No! No! Do not tell police, please! They must not know about my Lotus! Then her father find out!"

Kay said she would respect the woman's wishes, and do all she could to find Lotus herself. The girls said good-bye, and hurried to their car. Cara Noma's car was gone.

"I hope she didn't put a hex on our car," Betty said, giggling, as she climbed into the driver's seat.

Her joking remark relieved the tension, and the three girls gradually threw off the strange feeling which the Wongs' estate had cast over them.

"With all its beauty, I wouldn't want to live there," Wendy remarked as they drove away.

Kay's mother was upset by the time Kay got home.

She and Bill had finished their dinner and had begun to worry about her. As Kay told them what happened, the two of them shook their heads seriously.

"Mother, I didn't intend to go there without you," Kay said. "It all happened so suddenly."

"I'm not blaming you, dear," replied Mrs. Tracey. "But you must be careful."

"Bill," said Kay, "maybe you should look into Cara Noma's business. If she's a fake, she shouldn't be taking people's money."

Bill agreed, and said he would get in touch with the police in Lincoln to watch the woman.

"Oh! I forgot to tell you, Bill, I've found your desk!" said Kay. She told him where the desk was, and that she had been unable to look into it and get the money.

Bill offered to get in touch with the storage company first thing in the morning. Undoubtedly by the time she got home from school he would have an order for Kay to go take the money from the desk.

By noon Kay's curiosity got the best of her. She phoned her cousin at his office, and was startled to learn that before he had phoned, the desk had been taken away from the storage company.

"I didn't want to worry you about it, Kay," he said. "The people there insist they don't know where the desk went."

Kay groaned. Was Bill's money lost forever?

Not satisfied, Kay went to the storage company herself that afternoon. The uncooperative woman was not at the desk. Instead a girl who used to be a student at Carmont High School was in charge. Kay knew her well.

"Hello, Kay," said Sarah Bigelow. "What brings you here?"

Kay explained her problem. Sarah looked around. Then sure that nobody could hear her, she whispered, "That Mr. Trexler was here, and told the people not to dare tell anyone where he was taking the furniture. But I know."

"You do?" said Kay. "Where?"

"To a deserted house out on the road to Lincoln."

"Sarah, you're an angel!" Kay said excitedly. "Thanks a million!"

She left the office and hurried back to Carmont High where Wendy and Betty were playing tennis. Just as they finished a game, she rushed up to them.

"Hey, I want you to go with me to an abandoned old house."

"Not me," said Wendy firmly. "Yesterday's adventure was enough for me."

But when Kay explained her reasons, both girls said they would go along with her. Fortunately Betty and Wendy had brought the family car that day, and the three girls set off in a few minutes.

The place was not hard to find. As Betty turned into the driveway of the old house, a man came out to the porch.

"That's Sidney Trexler!" Kay cried.

VIII

A Chinese Puzzle

As Kay and the twins drove up, Sidney Trexler's face took on a look of amazement. He started into the house. Then, evidently changing his mind, he came down the porch steps to meet them.

"What can I do for you?" he asked.

Kay explained that she had been trying for several days to find him. She had gone to the auction expecting to bid on the desk, which Mr. Trexler had claimed as his own. While looking it over before the sale, she had found a secret drawer and in fun had slipped some money into it.

"But later," Kay continued, "I discovered I'd taken a blank envelope from the drawer instead of the one containing my money."

Sidney Trexler's eyes opened wide. "You say there is a secret compartment in the desk?" he asked.

Kay nodded. "Didn't you know about it?"

Mr. Trexler confessed that he did not. Then with a peculiar sort of laugh, he said, "In return for your money, suppose you show me the secret compartment."

Going inside the house to where the desk was, Kay pressed the secret spring and the drawer flew open. As she retrieved the money, she asked Trexler where he had obtained the desk.

"It was made by a Mr. Joe Wong," the man replied.

The three girls were astonished. Never having heard what Mr. Wong's business was, Kay asked for more details. Sidney Trexler said Mr. Wong was a very fine craftsman and made only unusual pieces of furniture.

"He specializes in small items," he told them. "He doesn't make large pieces like this desk very often." He laughed again. "Just like Joe to put a secret compartment in a desk and not tell anybody about it. You were smart to find it."

"Thank you, Mr. Trexler," Kay said. Then, looking the man right in the eye, she asked, "Are you engaged to Lotus Wong?"

He seemed very startled at the question. His answer, however, was not what the girls expected.

"So you've heard I'm going to be married?"

"Yes. I understand to a Chinese princess."

Mr. Trexler laughed loudly. Then suddenly a cunning sort of look came into his eyes, and he remarked, "I'm not telling you the name of my fiancée. We'll just leave it that she's a Chinese princess."

"I should think," Wendy spoke up, "that you'd be pretty proud of it. Why won't you tell us her name?"

"I have my reasons," was all Mr. Trexler would say.

Turning abruptly, he indicated that the visit was at

an end and showed the girls to the door. Kay was disappointed not to receive a direct answer from him about Lotus Wong, but she knew it was futile to question him further. She also wished she had had a chance to talk about the jewel chest he had bought.

The girls started for home, happy that Kay had retrieved her lost money, even if she had not solved the mystery of the missing Lotus Wong.

"I suppose you'll follow Mr. Trexler," Wendy said to Kay.

"I'd like to," her friend answered, "but I don't see how that's possible. I have to go to school."

"And find out what the answer to X is," Betty added. "X being Lotus Wong."

Upon reaching home, Kay phoned Mrs. Wong and suggested that Lotus might be secretly engaged to the Mr. Trexler of whom she had spoken before.

"Lily Wong ask Cara Noma," she replied.

"Oh, no, please don't do that," Kay begged.

But before she finished the sentence, Mrs. Wong had hung up. Kay thought about the powerful influence the medium had on Mrs. Wong. How could Kay ever break it?

"What's this new complication in your life?" a voice behind her asked, and Bill came up to kiss her.

"Oh, hi," said Kay. "Well, I've accomplished what I went after!"

She opened her purse and pulled out the envelope containing his money. Lightheartedly she handed it over. Bill stared in disbelief.

"Well, little detective, suppose you tell me how you did it. I didn't think we'd ever get this money back."

As Kay was explaining it to him, she noticed the other envelope in her purse, which had come from Mr. Trexler's desk. For the first time she noticed that under the flap there were several Chinese symbols. Wondering if they had any significance, since the desk had been made by Mr. Wong, she decided to find out.

Next day after school, she went directly to Sun Sen's laundry, hoping that the old man was well and in his shop again.

As she reached the laundry, a boy stepped out of a car and started for the door.

"Hi, Kay!" he called. "Why didn't you tell me you were coming here? I'd have brought you over."

"Hi, Ronald," she said. "Why don't you drive me home instead?"

Ronald Earle was a high school friend of Kay's. She had known him for years and they went to all the local parties and dances together. He sometimes helped Kay solve mysteries. Now he said with a grin, "No new mysteries?"

Kay smiled. "Me, with no mysteries? . . . I'll tell you about the latest on the way home."

"I have a mystery of my own," he said. "This guy here who is taking Sun Sen's place has mixed up all the laundry. I've been trying for two days to get my own shirts."

The bored looking young Chinese man behind the counter waved his arms in a helpless gesture as Ronald once more asked for his bundle.

"This your tag. Shirt must belong Meester Earle," the attendant said.

Ronald opened the package and held up the shirt. He gave a snort.

"This is three sizes too big for me. Can you beat that?"

Kay giggled. "Maybe you've shrunk, Ronald."

"This shirt is big enough for a circus fat man!" the boy cried. "It's a regular tent!"

The Chinese boy shrugged. "Maybe you look for shirt," he said.

"That's a good idea," said Kay. "May we go into the back room and hunt?"

The clerk nodded indifferently. Kay and Ronald walked into a little room where the finished laundry was put. Seeing the large number of bundles which were there, they were dismayed. The tags were no help, for they were all written in Chinese.

"Let's give it up," said Ronald in a discouraged tone. "It would be easier to buy some new shirts."

"But we've only started to look," Kay laughed. "Come on, don't give up so easily."

Presently the young man came to see how they were making out. Seeing that their task was a hopeless one, he said, "Maybe you wait for Sun Sen. He come here soon."

"That settles it, Kay," said Ronald. "We'll go get a soda and come back later."

While they were in the soda shop, Kay told Ronald about the mystery she was working on. She asked him to keep the matter confidential, since Mrs. Wong did not want her husband to know yet that their daughter was missing. He promised to keep the secret, and said he was more intrigued with Cara Noma than he was with Lotus.

"She really sounds dangerous," he said. "I'd stay out of her way if I were you."

Half an hour later the pair walked down the street and turned the corner to go to Sun Sen's laundry again. To their amazement, there was a mob of people outside the laundry.

"What's going on?" Ronald asked in surprise.

"It looks like a riot!" exclaimed Kay. "Come on, Ronald, let's find out what's going on!"

IX

Angry Customers

As Kay and Ronald ran toward the laundry, they were able to figure out what was happening from the excited comments of the crowd. While Sun Sen was gone the clerk in charge had mixed up all the laundry. Now Sun Sen was back and the irate customers descended upon him; he was confused, and could do nothing.

"I know just how everyone feels," Ronald chuckled. "I don't like losing my property any more than they do."

"Let's see if we can do something to help," Kay suggested, "before Sun Sen's business is ruined completely."

Ronald went ahead, wedging a path through the crowd for Kay. They managed to get inside the building after considerable struggling and squeezing. Kay and Ronald spoke to the impatient mob assuring them their laundry would be returned.

Sun Sen was crouching fearfully behind his counter. In the face of this completely unexpected event he had forgotten nearly all the English he knew, and retorted to the angry demands of the customers in a torrent of Chinese. As Kay edged near him he saw her, and his wrinkled face brightened.

"You help me?" he pleaded. "Make people go away!"

Kay and Ronald took places behind the counter, eager to assist the man.

"Please," Kay requested. "If you'll all get into line, everyone will receive his laundry."

She and Ronald set to work, checking bundles and giving them out. Sun Sen finally was able to slip away into the back room. As Kay sorted the packages she chanced to glance toward the window, and saw Chris Eaton's angular face pressed against the glass.

"She would see us here!" Kay thought unhappily. "I bet she'll make up some story about this."

Kay had not misjudged her enemy. Quickly leaving the scene, Chris encountered a rowdy group of high school boys. She stopped them to tell her bit of news, saying that they should go to the laundry and see for themselves that Kay and Ronald were employed there.

About twelve or fifteen boys from Carmont High tried to push their way into the building. They crowded against the plate glass window, trying to attract the attention of Kay and Ronald. They jeered at the pair, who continued with their work, paying no attention to what was going on outside.

"You must be getting rich quick, Ronald," one of his classmates shouted, pounding on the glass.

"It's Pete Sparott and his gang who are causing all the trouble," Kay said irritably.

"Don't pay any attention to them, and they'll go away," Ronald answered quietly.

It was impossible, however, not to notice the troublemakers. Led by Pete, the unruly gang started chanting, "We want our laundry! We want our laundry!"

"We'll have to do something!" Kay cried. "They'll break the window if they don't stop."

She moved toward the front of the store with the intention of telling them to stop. At that moment a police car stopped in front of the building.

An officer ran toward the laundry, but the group of yelling boys surged against the window with such force that the plate glass shattered. Kay screamed as it crashed inward, sharp splinters hitting her on the forehead.

"Are you hurt?" cried Ronald, rushing to her. "You are! You've been cut!"

"It's nothing," said Kay shakily. "I don't even feel any pain so it must be only a scratch."

Miraculously no one else in the laundry had been struck by the flying bits of glass. The accident had frightened everyone however, and with a policeman on the scene, the crowd rapidly dispersed. Pete Sparott and his gang ran down an alley before they could be caught.

Ronald took out a clean handkerchief and wiped the blood from Kay's face. He was relieved to see that the cut was not a serious one.

Sun Sen had shuffled in from the back room. Wringing his hands despairingly, he said he would have to go out of business.

"It's not that bad," Kay assured him. "A new window, a broom, and everything will be all right."

Sun Sen cheered up a bit. He produced a broom

and Kay and Ronald helped him put the broken glass into a carton and set it in the rear yard. Then they hung a large sheet over the broken store front. "You so good to old Sun Sen," the laundryman said. "Kind thought bring kind deed."

"We'd better go now," said Kay.

"Of course," Ronald agreed instantly. "You look tired, Kay. Are you sure your head doesn't hurt?"

"Hardly at all. I'm all right."

As they were getting into Ronald's car, they heard their names called, and turned around to see Wendy and Betty hurrying toward them.

"Have you heard?" Betty cried indignantly, as they reached the sidewalk. "Chris Eaton is telling everybody that you——Kay, what happened to your forehead?"

"It looks like that scarlet cross Cara Noma placed on you!" Wendy exclaimed in horror. "It's the curse of the green cameo!"

Softly she recited:

> *"Behind the curtain of Life's Scene,*
> *There lurks a dark and throttling hand,*
> *Moved by a magic stone of green*
> *From some far-off, mysterious land."*

"You don't actually believe that, do you?" Kay asked.

"I'm beginning to think the green cameo does have a power," returned Wendy gravely. "So many things have happened to you since Cara Noma threatened you."

"Yes, but nothing caused by supernatural powers. This cut I received today was just an accident."

Kay refused to believe that Cara Noma had an ability to bring misfortune upon her. She also would not believe that the Wongs' troubles had been caused by their possessing the cameo.

Ronald drove the girls home. Dropping Kay off, he said to let him know if she needed any help with the mystery.

"I will," she promised, and ran into the house.

"Kay, what happened to you?" her mother cried, noticing the cut.

"A little accident," Kay admitted, and gave her mother an account of the afternoon's adventures.

"You certainly do manage to become involved in things," Mrs. Tracey sighed.

"But I'm not really getting anywhere with the mystery of Lotus Wong, Mother. There are clues, but they're so vague!"

"Something will turn up. And now dear, let's have dinner early. Bill's not coming home, so you'll have a chance to get your studying done and go to bed early."

By ten o'clock Kay was sound asleep, but she was awake early. While showering, she began to worry about old Sun Sen. Had the excitement at his shop been enough of a shock to cause a relapse?

Kay left early for school, so that she could stop at the laundry before taking the train to Carmont. To her relief Sun Sen was there and greeted her warmly.

"Sun Sen fix all bundles in mix-up," he said cheerily.

"Good. Now perhaps you can find Mr. Tracey's shirt."

He found it and Kay said either she or her cousin would pick it up later that day.

"I suppose there's no news of Lotus?" she asked.

Sun Sen looked down. "No. Sister very sad. Mr. Wong angry he not hear from daughter."

"He knows, then?"

"No. But Lotus write or call telephone every few day. Now she not do this."

Kay was about to hurry off for her train when she suddenly remembered what had brought her to the shop the day before. Taking the envelope with the Chinese symbols from her purse, she asked Sun Sen what they meant. He studied the faint writing a few moments.

"Strange message here," the old man replied at last. "This say, 'Boat has no curse on it.'"

X

Stagestruck

What boat had no curse on it, Kay wondered. She asked Sun Sen if the Wongs owned one.

"Before Wong move here he have boat," replied Sun Sen. "Not know now if he own it."

Kay thought about various possibilities. It was possible that Lotus Wong, afraid of the green cameo curse, had run away to the boat. But almost immediately, Kay decided that since Lotus attended college, she wouldn't be foolish enough to believe in superstitions.

Suddenly Kay looked at her watch. She just had time to make the train to Carmont. Thanking Sun Sen, she dashed out the door. The running girl had gone only a few feet, when she heard an automobile horn honking behind her.

"Kay!" cried Betty Worth from the wheel of her family's car. "Jump in quick!"

Kay got in, and as she flopped onto the seat, Wendy explained that because they were late they had borrowed the car. She had called Kay and found out that she had gone to Sun Sen's laundry.

"You're a lifesaver!" Kay said. "And since you have the car, could you go some place with me after school?"

"Sure thing," replied Betty. "Something to do with the mystery?"

Kay said she wanted to drive over to Lincoln College and talk to the dean and maybe some of Lotus Wong's friends. She had been hoping to do this for a few days, but hadn't been able to get there without a car.

"We were going shopping," Wendy said, "but we can skip that." She smiled. "We may have to go without summer clothes, but we'd rather find Lotus Wong."

Her eyes twinkling mischievously, Kay said, "How would you both like to go on a boat trip?"

The twins stared at her, then demanded to know what she was talking about. Kay told them about the strange message on the envelope which she had found in the desk Mr. Wong had made.

"Well," sighed Wendy, "I'm glad there's something connected with the Wongs that has no curse on it."

"Do you mean," Betty asked, "that if you find out the Wong's have a boat, you want us to go see it?"

"Yes—unless, of course, the boat is too far away."

Suddenly Betty giggled. "I hate to punch holes in your theory, Kay, but you know the boat might be a tiny one on a lily pond at the Wong estate."

"Yes," Wendy took up the teasing, "Mr. Wong may have made a toy boat once for Lotus."

Kay admitted there was a good chance they might be right, but in this mystery clues were so skimpy that she was not going to give up on the boat idea until she had tracked down its meaning.

Betty pulled into the school parking yard just five minutes before the bell rang. They dashed to their homeroom, out of breath, and the Wongs were forgotten.

Kay found the day's work absorbing and for several hours listened attentively to her teachers. But as soon as the closing bell rang, the whole problem of the Wongs came back to her, and she was in a hurry to start for Lincoln.

"All set?" Betty asked, meeting her in the corridor.

They had to wait a few minutes for Wendy, then drove to the college. Kay went first to the dean's office. Mrs. Rand, hearing from her secretary that Kay wished to talk to her about Lotus Wong, asked that Kay come in at once.

"Are you a friend of Lotus's from Brantwood?" she asked.

Kay explained that she had never met Lotus, but that she knew her mother and had promised to try to find her daughter. Mrs. Rand was astounded to learn that Mrs. Wong had not told her husband of the girl's disappearance.

The dean said that when Lotus had failed to return from a weekend away, she had phoned the Wong home and learned from the butler that Lotus had not been there. Mrs. Rand had then assumed she had gone home with one of her friends. The dean had just finished checking with Lotus's friends and found out that this was not the case, when a friend of Mrs. Wong's came to see her. The woman, saying she had heard that Lotus was missing, offered to convey the message to the Wongs.

"Do you know the woman who was here?" Kay asked. "Was she a relative of theirs?"

Mrs. Rand said the woman was not Chinese, but that she had been close to the family for years.

"She gave her name?" Kay asked.

"Oh, yes," Mrs. Rand replied. "She lives here in Lincoln. Her name is Mrs. Cara Noma."

Kay was not surprised to hear this.

"But you don't know anything about this woman personally?" Kay pursued her questioning.

"No," admitted the dean. "I must say I don't."

When Kay explained that the woman was a medium and that she had Mrs. Wong under her influence, Mrs. Rand was shocked. Worried because she had permitted this person to carry the message of Lotus's disappearance to the family, she said she would get in touch with Mr. Wong immediately.

"Oh, please don't do that!" Kay begged, and told her why Mrs. Wong was keeping the news from her husband.

Kay smiled at the dean.

"Mrs. Rand, I've had some luck in solving mysteries. Mrs. Wong has asked me to try to find Lotus. I think she probably ran away to escape marrying a man much older than herself. He's her father's choice, not hers."

"I see," the dean said. "Knowing Lotus as I do, however, she seemed very loyal to her parents and that didn't occur to me. I do have another idea about why she might have run away."

"Would you mind telling me what it is?" Kay asked eagerly.

"Not at all. After Lotus's disappearance, I talked with several of her friends about it. They told me that Lotus was stagestruck. They think she may have gone off to try joining some theater company."

"Has Lotus been studying drama here?" Kay asked.

"Yes. She was in a drama class and appeared in a few short plays."

"I'd like to speak to some of Lotus's friends," Kay said. "Could you tell me where their rooms are?"

Mrs. Rand gave directions to Ivy Hall, saying, however, that Lotus's friends were probably on the athletic field at this time of day. Kay thanked the dean for her help and went to get Betty and Wendy.

The three girls walked to Ivy Hall and looked first for a Janet Brown. Fortunately, she was in her room studying.

"We all feel terrible about Lotus's disappearance," she said, after hearing why the girls were there. "She's a great person and we all really like her."

Kay asked if Janet thought Lotus might have run away to avoid an arranged marriage.

"I don't know. Lotus never said anything about that."

"What's your theory?" Kay asked.

Janet shrugged. "There's one thing I'm sure of. She didn't plan to come back. Lotus sold a lot of things she had in her room, including a beautiful jewelry box."

"Did she tell you she was going to sell them?" asked Kay.

"No, but a couple of the girls saw them for sale in shops downtown. We think she ran away to try to get into the theater. She used to rehearse different roles in her room every night."

Kay asked Janet to take her to the room Lotus had lived in. She searched carefully for clues, and finally came to what she thought was a good one.

It was a program from a Chinese theater. Kay

noticed it was located in Long Point, not far from Lincoln. Happy that she had picked up at least a small bit of information, Kay thanked Janet and the three girls went back to their car.

"Maybe we're getting some place now," Kay said, as they started for Brantwood. "Let's stop at Lotus Gardens. I'd like to tell Mrs. Wong what I've learned and see if she can give me any more help."

"How could she help?" asked Wendy.

"Through Cara Noma. You remember the medium was the one who broke the news to Mrs. Wong when I was in Sun Sen's laundry?"

"Yes."

"I have a hunch Cara Noma may be responsible for Lotus's disappearance."

"Buy why?"

"That's what we have to find out!"

XI

The Sinister Hand

<hr>

"Uh, oh," said Betty, as Kay and the twins entered the driveway of Lotus Gardens. "I think Mr. Wong is here."

A short, stout Chinese stepped from his car and walked up to the front door of the mansion.

"This certainly changes my plans," declared Kay. "I won't dare mention Lotus's disappearance, and I can't find out much about her interest in the theater without arousing her father's suspicions."

The girls couldn't figure out whether Wong didn't realize there was a car directly behind him or if he had just decided to ignore it. He took a key from his pocket and let himself in without turning around.

"He must be deaf," Betty said bluntly.

Kay wasn't sure whether they should stay. But since another whole day would go by before she could come again, Kay decided to take the chance. She rang the bell and Chang opened the door.

"You are here to see Mrs. Wong?" he asked without changing the immobile expression on his face. "I will ask if this is possible. Mr. Wong has just returned and usually does not like his wife to have visitors at this time."

"Oh, please don't bother her," Kay spoke up quickly.

"But I should like Mrs. Wong to see you if at all possible," Chang said, and hurried off.

"What did he mean by that?" Betty asked.

"I haven't the foggiest idea," Kay replied. "That man is a total mystery, as is his mistress."

Five minutes later both Mr. and Mrs. Wong came into the living room where the girls were waiting. Kay could tell at once that the woman was more like she had been in Sun Sen's laundry before she had received word of Lotus's disappearance. Perhaps she was no longer under Cara Noma's influence!

The small woman smiled graciously but did not offer to introduce the girls. With a pleading look at Kay, Lotus's mother said:

"You come from Lincoln College to see me? You are Lotus friend?"

Betty almost gave the secret away. Kay, however, looked at her friends quickly and they said nothing.

"We've just driven over from Lincoln," Kay said to Mrs. Wong. "We're on our way to Brantwood and thought we'd stop in and say hello to you."

A look of relief came over Mrs. Wong's face. She smiled and said, "So sweet of you young ladies. When you see Lotus again, tell my lovely flower not study too hard. Much study make many wrinkles."

The girls giggled, and told their hostess they guessed they would not study too hard themselves. They did not want to become wrinkled!

Just as Kay began to fear her visit was in vain with Mr. Wong in the room, he arose and said that he had some business to attend to in his den. If the young ladies would excuse him, he would go.

"My husband very busy man," said Mrs. Wong. "He work day and night." She smiled at him as he left the room.

She then summoned Chang and asked him to bring tea for all of them. It was not until they were sipping from dainty little bowls, and Mrs. Wong had checked with Chang to be sure that her husband was in his den, that she whispered:

"Have you brought me news of Lotus?"

By this time the Worth twins were in the spirit of the little intrigue. While Kay and Mrs. Wong talked in low voices, the two girls laughed and talked loudly about life at Lincoln College. Mrs. Rand was so nice and always knew how to handle the students' problems. But there was one spiteful old instructor——

Meanwhile, Kay had told Mrs. Wong what she had learned about her daughter from the dean and the students. The woman seemed both shocked and relieved at the thought that her daughter was trying to get on the stage. She asked if Kay could possibly go to Long Point and find out if Lotus were at the National Theater.

"I no write or telephone," said Mrs. Wong. "I think Mr. Wong believes something strange is going on. He get mad many times lately."

"Mrs. Wong," said Kay, "I'd like to ask you a very personal question. Does Mr. Wong know that Cara Noma comes here?"

A frightened look came over the Chinese woman's face and she shook her head. "Please not to tell Mr. Wong about Cara Noma," she begged.

"I have to be frank with you, Mrs. Wong," replied Kay. "I do not believe Cara Noma can do all the things for you that she said. She tells you that she is trying to find Lotus, and I believe she's perhaps responsible for Lotus running away."

Mrs. Wong almost dropped her bowl of tea. She looked at Kay wildly, and said she was sure the girl was wrong. Cara Noma was a person with supernatural powers, and she had been very helpful to Mrs. Wong for some time.

"Can you tell me how?" Kay asked.

"I cannot tell you, but Cara Noma good friend," was all Mrs. Wong would reveal.

Kay decided to change the subject. She asked whether it might be possible for her to see the green cameo which Mr. Wong had obtained in China.

Mrs. Wong hesitated, then got up. She went to an ornamental cabinet in the room, and pressed a secret spring at the back. The girls could hear something sliding, and a moment later the woman withdrew a small Chinese box.

"Maybe curse fall again when I show cameo," Mrs. Wong said. "I no look at it. You open and see."

Betty and Wendy had stopped chattering. Their eyes bulging, they looked on as Kay opened the box and took out a large, quaint cameo. The face of a beautiful woman was carved in relief on the delicate green stone. As the girls stared at it, the face seemed to come alive.

"The eyes are moving!" cried Wendy, terrified.

"Yes, and the woman is smiling!" said Betty in awe, for once not telling Wendy she was being silly.

Kay was also fascinated by the face on the cameo. It did seem to be smiling at them. Kay felt like she was being bewitched by the little object in her hand. She got up to give it back to Mrs. Wong.

The woman had moved off a little distance, and seated herself in a low chair near a heavy drapery. Her eyes were closed and she was muttering in Chinese.

Kay walked over and laid the mystic gem in her hand. As Kay stared at it, suddenly the drapery parted. A man's hand reached through and snatched the green cameo!

XII

An Oriental Play

Before Mrs. Wong opened her eyes, Kay had pulled the drape aside. To her amazement there was no door on the other side. Instead, there was a wall panel.

"It must have a secret opening!" Kay thought.

Turning to Mrs. Wong, she asked what was behind the panel. Mrs. Wong stared at her as if under a spell. Apparently she did not understand what Kay was talking about. Then she put her hand onto her forehead, and leaned back in the chair.

"Mrs. Wong! Don't you hear what I'm saying? Someone has stolen the green cameo!" Kay cried.

"No! No!" Mrs. Wong mumbled. "Curse come to house of Wong again!"

"Please, Mrs. Wong," Kay begged, "help me. Try to understand, someone has stolen the green cameo. We must find the man. How do I get on the other side of this wall?"

Her pleas fell on deaf ears. Mrs. Wong merely closed her eyes and swayed in her chair. "Lily Wong die! Lily Wong die!" she muttered.

"Let's get out of here—and quick!" Betty spoke up. "I've had enough of this crazy place."

But Kay was not giving up so easily. Dashing into the hall, she tried to figure out how to find the room which would join the wall through which the hand had reached. Her efforts were futile. Every door along the hallway was locked.

"If you insist," said Betty. "I'll help you look for the thief outside. He's probably gone off by this time."

The three girls hurried out the front door, and rushed to the side of the house where the mysterious room probably opened. They looked up at the windows. They were closed. No one was around, and they didn't hear the sound of a car.

"Oh, please, let's go," begged Wendy. "I'll see that smiling cameo in my dreams!"

By this time Kay had calmed down. She began to laugh, and Betty asked Kay what she was thinking.

"My first idea," said Kay, "is to agree with Wendy and go home."

Surprised and relieved, Betty and Wendy went with her to the car. It was not until they were out on the highway that Kay told them her impression of what had happened in the mysterious house. Mr. Wong had been listening all the time through a secret panel behind the drape. Kay even doubted that Mrs. Wong knew it was there. Either fearing that Kay intended to steal the green cameo, or wishing to teach his wife a lesson, the owner of this strange ornament had reached through and taken it.

"Then you mean it wasn't stolen at all?" asked Wendy, wide-eyed.

"It's only a guess," Kay replied. "But from the glimpse I had of Mr. Wong as he entered the house and the way he ignored us, I wouldn't trust him very far."

Wendy thought that Kay should give up the whole idea of trying to find Lotus Wong. The entire business was too spooky.

"But you'll admit it's not dangerous," Kay spoke up.

"What about your adventure in that strange room with the tinkling bells and the incense," Wendy said.

"I don't believe the Wongs had anything to do with that. I'm sure it was Cara Noma who slapped me and started the incense burning."

"Well," said Betty, "if you're determined to go on with this mystery, count me in. When do we go to Long Point to that Chinese theater?"

Kay replied that she was going as soon as she possibly could. But the next day in school her plans had to be changed. The principal announced a delegation of foreign visitors to the United States was making the rounds of selected schools to see various kinds of work. Carmont High School had been chosen to put on a short play.

"There are only a few days in which we can rehearse and get everything ready," the principal said. "With this in mind, I would like everyone who is interested to report to the auditorium after classes today. I particularly recommend that those who have been in plays before and feel they can learn their lines quickly apply for the parts."

The corridors buzzed with excitement as the students filed out to classes. There was speculation about those who would try out. But there was no doubt that Kay would compete. She had often appeared in school plays, and learned lines easily.

Later in the day the students were told that those chosen for the parts would be excused from classes to learn their lines. Kay was glad to hear this because now, if she were fortunate enough to get a role, she could continue her work on the mystery and drive over to Long Point to look for Lotus Wong.

Several boys and girls, excitedly discussing their chances, gathered in the auditorium. Copies of the play were handed out by Mr. Reynolds, the drama coach. Kay was very surprised when she discovered that it had an oriental background and was entitled, *"The Pagoda Mystery."*

Betty Worth and Jean Scott also tried out for the main female part, that of a beautiful maiden. But because of her recent experiences at the Wong home, Kay spoke her lines with special feeling and proved her familiarity with Chinese customs and people. Therefore, the leading role was given to her. Betty and Jean, though naturally a little disappointed, were happy Kay had gotten the part. But Chris Eaton, jealous because she had not been chosen, said in a loud, scornful voice:

"Who couldn't get that role—after working in a Chinese laundry!"

Kay was annoyed, but ignored the rude remark.

The tryouts concluded, the rest of the cast was chosen. To Kay's dismay, Pete Sparott received the male lead opposite her.

"It would be much more fun if Ronald had the part," she thought. "Acting with Pete will be a pain."

Ronald, however, was too busy with sports to be allowed to try out. Both Betty and Jean were given secondary roles. Chris received a minor part—so minor that it consisted of only a few lines.

"Rehearsals will begin tomorrow morning," Mr.

Reynolds explained. "We must work very hard if the play is to be a success."

"Are we going to have Chinese clothes and scenery?" Betty asked.

"Yes. If any of you has access to oriental props, costumes or furniture, please speak to me about it."

Kay spoke up. "I think I can get some things," she said. "I'm sure a Chinese acquaintance of mine will lend us some furniture. Carved chairs, tables, wall hangings, screens and things like that."

"Just what we need," Mr. Reynolds said enthusiastically. "We would really appreciate it, Kay, if you could get them for us."

"I'll do my best."

"I can bring something really fine," Chris interrupted in smug tones. "A handsome Chinese lamp! It's worth hundreds of dollars!"

All the students smiled. They knew that Chris was just trying to attract attention.

"This lamp has a strange story behind it," Chris went on with an air of importance. "Years ago——"

"I'm sorry, but we haven't time to hear it now," the coach cut in.

Chris frowned and was silent. During the following morning she passed a great many notes to Pete Sparott. At lunchtime they walked slowly back and forth together in the school grounds.

"Kay isn't the right type to play a Chinese maiden," Chris protested to Pete. "If she weren't the teacher's favorite, the part would have been given to me."

"I'd rather play opposite you any time," Pete assured her loyally.

"I know how we can fix it that way," suggested Chris slyly.

"How?"

"Oh, just by fixing it so that on the night of the play Kay will be—let's say—unable to act."

"What could we do?"

"I'll think of something good, Pete. Leave it to me."

"But," Pete said warily, "even if Kay can't take the part, you'd never get it. They'd just postpone the performance."

"Not if I knew the lines," Chris smiled. "This is my plan, Pete. I'll learn Kay's part and we'll practice all her scenes together. Then, on the night of the play, we'll be so perfect in our roles that Mr. Reynolds won't be able to refuse to let me have the part."

"Not a bad idea," Pete agreed. "It's worth a try."

Unaware of the two plotting against her, Kay talked enthusiastically to Betty about the furniture she hoped to borrow from Mrs. Wong. During the conversation neither of them noticed that Chris and Pete were near and listening closely.

"I'll drive out to Lotus Gardens tomorrow," Kay told Betty.

"We must get there first," Chris whispered to her companion. "We'll go tonight."

The pair set off for Lotus Gardens in Pete's station wagon as soon as the meeting was over. When Chang arrived at the gate, attracted by the loud honking of Pete's car horn, brazen Chris calmly told the servant that the principal of Carmont High had sent her to obtain some Chinese articles which were needed as props in a school play.

"Did Mrs. Wong give her permission?" Chang inquired doubtfully.

"I'm sure she did," answered Chris.

The servant reluctantly admitted the couple to the

house and said he would get his mistress. As he returned, saying she could not see them, Joe Wong appeared in the doorway.

"What does this mean, Chang?" he demanded sternly, as he caught Chris with priceless vases under her arms, and Pete with a chair.

"Kindly tell me what you do with my possessions."

Even bold Chris was shocked at his unexpected entrance, and disconcerted by his angry look. But she pulled herself together and assured him that she thought the school principal had made the arrangements. She and Pete were to pick out the pieces and take them away.

In spite of his anger, a cunning look came into Mr. Wong's eyes. His attitude changed and he said he would let the two take the pieces. His furnishings, he added, were a source of pride and to display them before an audience would be a pleasure.

Chris and Pete chose a tea table, a screen, two vases, and a lamp, while Mr. Wong looked on with an impassive face.

Chris was so pleased at the success of her scheme that she thanked Mr. Wong effusively. He bowed stiffly.

"Offer my regards to your principal," he said, "and impress on him that these articles are of great value. They must be guarded with care."

Chris and Pete lost no time in placing their acquisitions in the station wagon, and drove off.

"Just wait until Kay Tracey comes here and finds out we beat her to it!" Chris laughed. "She'll be furious!"

XIII

The Strange Message

The rehearsal was just about to start the next day when Kay dashed into the auditorium.

She stopped and stared in surprise. The stage was beautifully set up as a Chinese room. Where had the furniture come from?

"Hurry, Kay!" Mr. Reynolds called out. "You come on stage in a moment."

Kay rushed through the door and up onto the stage from the rear. The first thing she noticed was an exquisite vase. It was exactly like one the Wongs had!

"That was your cue," Mr. Reynolds said, somewhat annoyed.

"Oh, I'm sorry," said Kay. "I was so amazed to see this furniture, I wasn't paying attention."

Kay wanted to ask where the things had come from, but she didn't dare delay the rehearsal any longer. Mr. Reynolds asked the speaker before her to repeat his lines, then Kay spoke her part without hesitation.

As Mr. Reynolds prompted the next speaker, he took a moment to praise Kay for having learned her part so quickly. At the end of an hour he declared that for a first rehearsal everything had gone very well, and thanked the students for their cooperation.

"We have a long way to go though," he said. "I want all of you to be letter perfect by our next rehearsal. This is a difficult project, but I'm sure we can succeed."

As soon as the drama coach had dismissed the students, Kay hurried to him and asked where the stage setting had come from. When she learned that Chris Eaton and Pete Sparott had borrowed the furnishings from Mr. and Mrs. Joe Wong, Kay was thunderstruck. She turned to Chris, asking:

"Do you know the Wongs personally?"

"You're not the only one who gets around," said Chris flippantly. "You have the leading part in the play now, but don't be too sure you're going to keep it."

"What do you mean?" Kay demanded.

Chris smirked and merely quoted, "There's many a slip 'twixt the cup and the lip." She flounced off, joining Pete. The two left the auditorium giggling.

"Can you beat that?" Betty asked. "How in the world did Chris get this stuff from the Wongs?"

Kay shrugged. "I'm going to call their house and ask about something else. Maybe they'll tell me."

Noticing that the beautiful objects apparently were going to be left on the auditorium stage, Kay became worried. She spoke to Mr. Reynolds about it, saying she was afraid that they might be broken, or even stolen.

"I agree with you," Mr. Reynolds remarked. "Chris said she would be responsible for them. I understood she was going to keep the smaller pieces at her home."

Kay ran after Chris, but she had disappeared. She returned to the auditorium, and offered to take the vases to her home until the next day. Mr. Reynolds thanked her but suggested instead she help him carry them to the principal's office, where they could be locked up until they were needed. Betty helped also. Then the two girls went home.

As they rode on the train toward Brantwood, the girls could talk of nothing else but the furniture which Chris had managed to obtain.

"Did you hear how she got it?" Kay asked Betty.

Betty shook her head. She was sure that Chris didn't know the Wongs. But how she had succeeded in borrowing the things was a mystery.

"I'll find out from Mrs. Wong," Kay said, "I'm going to phone her and ask if by any chance there are any Chinese costumes of Lotus's that I could use."

"Oh, ask her for a suit for me, too, will you?" Betty asked.

As soon as supper was over, Kay went to the phone. Chang answered at the Wong home. After Kay had asked for his mistress, he went off but returned in a few seconds.

"I am sorry, Miss Tracey," he said. "But neither Mr. nor Mrs. Wong wishes to speak to you. If you will leave a message, I shall give it to them."

Kay was shocked. "Did I understand you right? They don't want to speak to me?"

"That's what I said."

"But why?" cried Kay.

Chang did not reply. Kay repeated her question. Finally the butler said, "I do not know, miss."

On a sudden hunch Kay asked the man if Cara Noma was there. If so, she would like to speak to her. Again there was a silence of several seconds. Then finally Chang said:

"I will find out."

He came back in a few moments and continued, "No one here wishes to speak to you, Miss Tracey." With this, he hung up.

Kay was sure Cara Noma was at the Wongs, because Chang had not denied her presence there. This might mean that Mr. Wong was not at home, and Cara Noma had told Chang what to tell Kay.

The girl sat thoughtfully by the telephone, then dialed Lotus Gardens again. Once more Chang answered.

Kay identified herself and explained, "I'd like to ask you some questions, since Mr. and Mrs. Wong don't want to speak with me."

"I never talk about my employers," was Chang's stiff reply.

"But you did say you would deliver a message to them," Kay reminded him.

"That's right," the butler replied.

Kay said she had two questions: First of all, she would like to borrow a Chinese dress for herself and another for a friend if Mrs. Wong would lend them. Her second question was, did the Wongs own a boat?

"Your message will reach them," Chang offered.

"Can you answer my question about the boat?" Kay asked insistently.

"I will deliver your message," was the evasive response.

When Kay discussed the matter with her mother, Mrs. Tracey suggested that perhaps Lotus Wong had come home and the Wongs didn't care to discuss the matter any further with Kay.

"Well, you'd think they'd at least thank me for what I've done," said Kay. Her mother smiled, advising Kay not to expect thanks for what she did. People often had reasons which made it hard for them to express their gratitude.

Kay felt uneasy about this new situation, but she decided to turn her attention to the school play. Perhaps Mrs. Wong would change her mind.

While Kay was dressing on Monday morning, her mother brought a special delivery letter to her room. She did not recognize the handwriting, although the letter had been mailed in Brantwood. Tearing it open, she read a bold, printed message:

"Do not play the part of a Chinese maiden or misfortune will follow you."

XIV

A Mysterious Refusal

"What's the matter, Kay," Mrs. Tracey asked her daughter. "You look as if a ghost had sent the letter."

"I guess one did," Kay answered, and handed the message to her mother.

"Do you think that Cara Noma wrote it?" she asked.

"No, Mother, I don't think so. I think it was Chris Eaton."

"What makes you say that?"

Kay replied that if Cara Noma had done it, she would have put something in it about the green cameo or the bad luck which she was trying to transfer to the girl. Chris didn't know anything about this, and therefore could not use it.

"I'm sure if Chris knew anything about it, she wouldn't let that slip by her."

Kay said that she was not worried about the message and was going to try to find out if Chris had sent it.

"You know, Mother, Chris wants my part very badly, and I wouldn't be surprised if she tried a few tricks to get it."

Kay tucked the note into her bag and ran downstairs to breakfast. Bill was already there. She told him about the note, and he agreed it was probably Chris's doing.

When he heard that the Wongs did not wish to speak to Kay, a frown creased his forehead.

"It's amazing how people can be so friendly one minute and so unfriendly the next," he remarked. "That's not good business. And Mr. Wong is evidently a pretty good businessman to have acquired the money he has."

Mrs. Tracey laughed. "That's a typical lawyer's point of view," she said. "Bill, don't forget that Mrs. Wong is under the influence of a medium, and that's enough to make anyone unbusinesslike."

"Have it your way, Kathryn," Bill laughed, rising from the table. "I'm glad nobody around here is under her influence. I certainly enjoyed this breakfast."

Before Kay left the house, she telephoned the Wong residence, but received the same answer from Chang as she had the evening before.

"Well," she shrugged, "if they won't talk to me, I can't borrow a costume from them. I'll have to see about renting one. I'll tell Betty."

Kay met the Worth twins at the station and showed them the threatening note. Both were sure Chris was behind it.

"If she finds out you haven't paid any attention to it," said Betty, "you'd better watch out. Chris is bound to try something else."

Seeing Chris Eaton on the station platform, the girls deliberately followed her and took seats directly behind her in the train. Winking at Betty, Kay presently said in a rather loud voice, "The funniest thing happened. I received a letter in the mail and I think the writer said just the opposite from what she intended to."

As she had expected, Chris turned her head slightly so that she could get every word. Kay went on:

"The note said, 'Do not play the part of the Chinese maiden badly, or misfortune will follow you.'"

Chris turned all the way around in the seat, an odd expression on her face. Before she thought, the girl said, "The note didn't say that at all."

Kay and the Worths giggled. Chris had been caught!

"Why, Chris," said Kay, pretending surprise, "the letter wasn't signed. Do you often send letters you don't put your name on?"

Chris blushed to the roots of her hair. She stammered that she had had nothing to do with it. She had heard other people in school talking about writing to Kay.

"If you want to know what people are saying about you," said Chris in a rather loud voice, "they think you're terrible in the part. The sooner you get out, the better!"

She rose quickly from the seat and took another one farther forward in the coach.

"Well, that didn't take long," Betty commented.

"Just the same, Kay, you'd better be careful of

Chris," said Wendy. "You know she doesn't like to be crossed." She quoted:

> *"A wounded vampire in disgrace*
> *Will turn and fly into thy face."*

Chris kept out of their way the rest of the day. Except for classes and a short period during lunch hour in the cafeteria, they did not see her until rehearsal time.

Kay knew her part perfectly and spoke her lines well, but Pete Sparott did everything he could to mix her up. In several of the dialogues between them, he spoke his own lines with accents not intended by the author of the play. He seemed to be trying to get some message across which was not part of *The Pagoda Mystery*.

"Pete, will you stop it?" Kay said in a low voice. "You're just ruining it."

"I'll say it any way I want," the boy replied.

But the coach was aware that something was not right. Finally Pete's rashness provoked the coach, who said:

"I can't understand your attitude, Pete. Unless you do better, I'll have to replace you with someone who shows more interest."

Instead of looking at the coach, Pete glanced directly at Chris. Kay was sure that she had started the whole thing, and that Pete didn't like being reprimanded for it. After that he spoke his lines perfectly and the rehearsal went very well.

Mr. Reynolds spoke to Kay and Betty after the rehearsal about their costumes, reminding them that they had not given him an order for them.

"The play is only two days away," he said. "We haven't much time left."

"I was hoping to borrow costumes from the same people who own this furniture," Kay told him. "I'll try once more. If I don't find out anything today, I'll let you know."

As she left the auditorium, Kay saw Ronald Earle coming in from the athletic field. A sudden thought came to her, and she went up to him and asked if he would make a phone call for her.

"Sure. Where to, Kay?"

She explained that she had tried twice to call the Wongs and had been told that they did not want to talk to her. Feeling that someone else was behind this, she thought that maybe if Ronald made the call and got Chang on the wire, he might let Ronald speak to Mrs. Wong. The two went to a telephone and Ronald dialed Lotus Gardens.

"Hello! Is this the Wong home? This is Mr. Earle. I would like to speak to Mrs. Wong."

"I will see," said Chang.

He returned in a few moments, saying that his mistress wished to know who Mr. Earle was. Ronald asked that Chang hold the wire a moment. He turned to Kay and whispered:

"Who am I?"

Kay could hardly stifle a giggle, but she said, "You work in Sun Sen's laundry."

Grinning, Ronald turned back to the phone and told this to Chang. The butler went off again for a few moments, and finally came back, saying Mrs. Wong would come on the phone. When the woman arrived, it was Kay to whom she spoke, not Ronald. The girl said she had been trying for days to speak to her and had some things she wished to talk over.

"No one tell me this," was Mrs. Wong's surprised answer. "I be glad to see you at once."

"I'll be there as soon as I can," Kay said.

After she had hung up, Kay asked Ronald if by any chance he had his car with him and wasn't busy.

"At your service, Kay," he replied cheerfully. "The limo waits for you."

After Ronald changed his clothes, the two started off.

When they arrived at Lotus Gardens, Kay was surprised that Mrs. Wong herself opened the door. She was very cordial to Ronald and invited him to wait in the living room while she and Kay had a private talk. She escorted the girl to the dimly-lighted room where Kay had been overcome by the incense. They sat on a blue damask sofa.

"This great mystery what you tell me on phone," Mrs. Wong said.

Kay asked whether Mrs. Wong had given Chang orders that she didn't want to speak to Kay again. The woman shook her head violently.

"I not say such thing," she said. Then a look of fear came over her face. "You have something important to tell me—about my Lotus perhaps?"

"Nothing new. But I would like to know, does your husband own a boat that——"

Kay gasped, as Mrs. Wong sank back in a faint.

XV

Hypnotized

Kay turned around and saw Cara Noma in the doorway!

Without waiting to help Mrs. Wong, Kay made a leap for the door and slammed it in the medium's face. Seeing a key in the lock, she turned it.

"That woman was putting Mrs. Wong in a trance!" Kay thought wildly. "But she won't continue!"

Kay had read and heard a lot about hypnotism. Although she had never tried using it on anyone, she was tempted to do so now. If she could only put some helpful ideas into Mrs. Wong's head while she was under the spell!

"I hope nothing goes wrong!" the girl thought as she moved toward the woman, who lay still on the sofa. Kay sat down beside her and said in a slow, calm voice:

"Cara Noma is not a true friend of yours. She is only trying to get your money."

After Kay had repeated this several times, she went on, "Lotus is eager to see her mother. But she is being kept away by the wicked Cara Noma."

Kay kept saying this over and over. Mrs. Wong moved slightly. Was she coming out of the trance? Kay watched her carefully, but the woman did not open her eyes. The girl decided to go on.

"Learn to trust good people, Mrs. Wong. One who wants to help you very much is Kay Tracey. Listen to what she says and follow her advice."

As she was repeating these words for the fifth time, Mrs. Wong's eyelids fluttered open. She looked dazed, but after rubbing her slender fingers over her eyes, she became fully awake. She spoke several words in Chinese. Then, realizing Kay was there, she said:

"What happen to Lily Wong?"

Kay helped the woman to sit up, saying that apparently she was not feeling well. She had fainted, but was all right now.

"Lily Wong in good health," the Chinese woman insisted, "but faint many time lately."

"Perhaps you should see a doctor," Kay advised.

A strange look crossed Mrs. Wong's face, then she replied with a smile, "I will see doctor, Miss Tracey. You very good friend. I always listen to your advice."

Kay was thrilled! Her message must have penetrated to Mrs. Wong's subconscious mind!

"Oh, if it will only last!" the girl thought.

She decided not to bring up the subject of the boat again. It might undo the good work she had accomplished. Instead, she said she had come to borrow a costume for the school play.

Mrs. Wong smiled. "Come to Lotus room and choose costume," she invited.

Mrs. Wong stood up and Kay followed her through the hall and up the stairway. Lotus Wong's bedroom was the most fascinating one Kay had ever seen. The Chinese furniture in it, all made by Mr. Wong, his wife explained, was beautifully carved. A heavy Chinese rug in tones of dark blue and tan lay on the floor. Rich silk drapes with a Chinese garden scene embroidered on them hung at the two windows. There was a delicious perfume in the air.

"Please to open Lotus closet," Mrs. Wong said. "Tell me, what part you play?"

While Kay looked over the many beautiful silk trousers and coats which hung in a row, she told the woman a little of the story of the play and the part she was playing. Mrs. Wong nodded her head and smiled.

"This play translation from Chinese," she remarked. "When Lily Wong young girl she play same part."

Kay was thrilled. On a sudden impulse, she crossed the room and threw her arms around Mrs. Wong.

"Please go through the lines for me," she requested. "Even if you say the words in Chinese I can watch your motions and play my part better."

Without questioning Kay, Mrs. Wong sat on the bench of the dressing table and took a pose. Then she began her lines, raising and lowering her arms gracefully and using her eyelids with very fine effect. She seemed to have thrown off all her fears. Even her face looked younger.

Kay watched in fascination. When Mrs. Wong finished, the girl said:

"Would you mind, Mrs. Wong, if I say the lines in English, and you coach me in the movements?"

"Lily Wong glad to," she replied.

Kay took the same position on the bench and did her best to imitate the motions as she spoke the lines. The result was a dismal failure. Mrs. Wong giggled like a girl.

"Maybe hard to make motions with English words," she said kindly. "I show you again."

The rehearsal went on for nearly half an hour before Kay was able to imitate the dainty movements of Mrs. Wong's long fingers. Fluttering her eyelids was more of a task, and this took another fifteen minutes of practice.

"When you have makeup on like Chinese girl," said Mrs. Wong enthusiastically, "everyone in theater think you Chinese maiden."

Kay thanked her for all her trouble. She picked out two costumes, one for herself and one for Betty, and then said she must go. It suddenly occurred to her that Ronald Earle was waiting in the living room.

Mrs. Wong accompanied Kay to the first floor. Kay was not surprised to find that Ronald had left the living room.

"I guess my friend got tired of waiting," she said. "He's probably out in the car listening to the radio."

Mrs. Wong apologized for having kept Kay so long, but the girl said she was sure Ronald did not mind waiting. He was probably listening to a baseball game.

"Mrs. Wong, would you like to come to the play?" Kay asked. "It's at the Carmont High School Wednesday evening."

"I speak Mr. Wong," the woman replied. "Lily Wong like to go, but sometime husband say she stay home with him."

"I see." Kay smiled, then she leaned over and whispered, "I want to talk to you about several things.

But there's no time to now. I think I have a good clue about your daughter. As soon as the play's over, I'm going to find out."

"You are very dear person," said Mrs. Wong. "I feel much better. Lily Wong have many headaches lately and cry too much. Cara Noma try to make me feel better. No luck."

Kay held her breath as she waited for Mrs. Wong to go on. To Kay's delight Mrs. Wong said:

"No more pay attention to Cara Noma. Lily Wong think green cameo curse not so bad. Curse come only to people who believe in it."

Kay hugged the woman. Her own little trick of hypnotism had worked!

The two walked outside and stared in surprise. No one was in the car!

"Ronald must be walking around the gardens," said Kay. "I'll look for him."

Mrs. Wong returned to the house and Kay set out on a search for Ronald. But though she wandered around for several minutes looking, she saw no sign of him. Finally Kay came to the conclusion that he was still in the Wong residence. Ringing the bell, she asked Chang if he had seen the youth.

"I do not understand," said the butler.

Kay explained that she and Ronald Earle had come to the house together. She had left him in the living room while she went upstairs with Mrs. Wong. Now Ronald did not seem to be around.

"If he is in the house, I know nothing about it," said Chang coldly.

"Then I'll have to look for him myself," said Kay, stepping into the hall.

Mrs. Wong was not in sight, so Kay walked down

the hall by herself. All the doors were open. She peered into the various rooms, but Ronald was not in any of them.

"Where could he have gone?" Kay thought apprehensively.

Cara Noma might have introduced herself to Ronald. After Kay's experience with the incense, there was no telling what might have happened to Ronald.

XVI

Conspiracy

━━━━━━━━━━━◆━━━━━━━━━━━

Suddenly, through a window, Kay saw Ronald walking up the driveway. She raced outside.

"Ronald! I was worried about you. Where have you been?"

"Tell you as soon as we're on the road," he whispered.

They got into the car, and as soon as they were a little distance from Lotus Gardens, Ronald began his story. He had gotten tired of waiting in the house, and had decided to go outside and walk through the gardens.

"I was just coming around the side of the house," Ronald continued, "when suddenly a door burst open and a woman dashed out. From what you'd told me, I was sure she was Cara Noma. I played detective and ran down the road after her."

"Where did she go?" Kay asked excitedly.

"Cara Noma jumped into a car and drove off," Ronald replied.

Seeing a look of disappointment cross Kay's face, he reached into his pocket and brought out a ten dollar bill.

"Your friend Cara Noma dropped this. How about returning it?" He handed the bill to Kay.

At first Kay fingered it absently. Then suddenly she noticed that the picture of the old automobile on the back was blurred!

"Ronald, this is a counterfeit! Exactly like those that Betty and Wendy had!" Kay cried. "The bills their mother brought from San Francisco!"

Ronald let out a low whistle.

"How in the world did Cara Noma get one?" Then he added wryly, "That woman really gets around."

Kay admitted it was possible that Cara Noma had been to California and picked up the counterfeit bill. On the other hand, it was also possible that these counterfeits were being circulated in the area of Brantwood!

"I'm going to report this to the Secret Service," she said.

When Ronald dropped Kay at her home, she told Bill, who offered to take care of the report for her.

"We'd better examine every ten dollar bill we get," he commented.

Kay laughed. "That won't be hard for me," she said. "I rarely have one."

At dinner she told her mother and the lawyer about her attempt at hypnotism. They both gasped, then broke into laughter.

"What on earth will you try next?" her mother asked, shaking her head.

"This Cara Noma sounds like a slick operator," remarked Bill. "If you can get the better of her, Kay, you'll deserve a medal."

Kay asked him if she should try to contact Cara Noma and return the bill.

"No, Kay," he declared firmly. "That isn't necessary."

He added that since the money was no good to the medium, it should be turned over to the proper authorities.

"If you happen to see Cara Noma, you'd better ask her where she got it, though," he said. "The Secret Service would want to know if the bills are being circulated near Brantwood."

After dinner Kay put on the two Chinese costumes, asking her family's opinion on which one she should wear in the play. They decided on a pure white one, embroidered in beautiful pink flowers and green leaves. The other, of dark blue, they thought would be perfect for Betty. Kay called her friend on the phone and told her about the costume.

"Oh, wonderful!" Betty cried. "I'll be right over."

It was late before Kay settled down to studying, but she was up in plenty of time next morning to catch an early train to school. To her surprise, Chris Eaton was in the same car. Since Chris usually took the latest possible train, Kay wondered why she was so early today.

Kay found out when she reached the Carmont station. Pete Sparott was there waiting for Chris and handed her a small package, which she slipped into a pocket of her dress. Neither of them saw Kay, who was surprised by their friendliness. "I guess they've found out they're two of a kind," Kay decided.

Upon reaching school, she went to the library for a special assignment she had not had time to do the day before. The school hours seemed to pass quickly, and before Kay knew it, rehearsal time had arrived. The Chinese objects were in their proper places when she reached the auditorium.

"I hope there will be no trouble today," Mr. Reynolds said, looking Pete Sparott squarely in the eye.

To Kay's relief, Pete played his opening lines well. Kay was superb in her part. As the young actors were given a breathing spell, Mr. Reynolds walked up to her. Smiling, he said:

"Kay, you have certainly learned a great deal about Chinese mannerisms. Where did you acquire the art of using your hands so beautifully and fluttering your eyelids that way?"

Kay confessed that Mrs. Wong had coached her. Mr. Reynolds was amazed to hear that the woman had once played the same part in China.

"She should come and see you in her role," he said. Then he called, "Everyone back on stage."

Soon Kay noticed that Chris Eaton, who had seated herself in the front row of the auditorium, was exchanging glances with Pete. Now and then the two would look in her direction.

"Watch out for sneaky tricks," Betty whispered in Kay's ear as she was called to the stage.

Pete seemed more keyed up than usual. He rattled off his lines so quickly that several times the coach was forced to ask him to speak more slowly.

"You seem eager to get through," commented Mr. Reynolds.

"Oh, no, sir," Pete denied, but Kay saw him wink at Chris.

From the wild look in Pete's eyes she suspected trouble ahead. Presently he began to mix up her cues and, in several instances, hopelessly confused her. He jerked her around roughly whenever his role gave him the slightest pretext for doing so. Kay finally protested.

"Oh, quit complaining," Pete sneered. "We need a little action in this play."

The scene reached its climax. Pete said, "'Maiden, you have betrayed my trust! Go! Go!'"

As Kay moved toward him pleadingly, he caught her firmly by the arm and pushed her backward with all his strength. She tried desperately to stop herself, but lost her balance and crashed heavily into a carved chair!

This was too much! Kay, indignant, turned toward the coach, intending to announce that she would no longer play opposite Pete. Before she could speak, however, Mr. Reynolds walked over to him.

"You're through, Sparott," he said angrily. "I won't tolerate your conduct any longer. Leave your costume in the dressing room and get out right now!"

Everyone was stunned. Finally Kay, rubbing a bruised elbow, found her voice.

"Who will play Pete's part?"

Mr. Reynolds reflected a moment. "The only boy in school who has been in several plays and might learn the part quickly is Ronald Earle. I'll ask the principal if he would make a special concession, even though Earle is carrying all the points he's allowed to."

The permission was obtained and Ronald summoned from the athletic field. He was overwhelmed to hear what had happened. Mr. Reynolds pointed out the lines in a copy of the play.

"Do you think you could take the role?" the coach asked.

"With only one rehearsal?" Ronald smiled dubiously. "I'm afraid I'd spoil the play."

"No, you wouldn't," Kay interposed quickly. "You can do it, Ronny. I'll help you if you forget your lines, I know most of them myself."

"What do you say?" Mr. Reynolds urged.

"I'll do the best I can," Ronald promised, though a bit reluctantly.

"Good! We'll go through the whole play. You read the lines. Then you'll have twenty-four hours to memorize them. I'll arrange for you to have a free day tomorrow to devote to them."

"Thank you very much. I'll dig right in!"

The rehearsal went on, with everyone pleased but Chris Eaton. She spoke her own few lines listlessly. After the rehearsal was over, Betty said to Kay:

"You know, it was funny the way Chris imitated you."

"What do you mean?" Kay asked in surprise.

"All the time she was offstage and you were on, she was using her hands just the way you do and saying every word right after you. It was hysterical to watch her flutter her eyelids."

"Why—almost as if she's learning my part!" Kay exclaimed in amazement.

"It does look that way," Betty replied. "But she never could play it like you do."

It was hard for Kay to keep her mind on classroom work the following day. Would the final bell never ring? At last it was time for rehearsal and Mr. Reynolds quickly went through certain sections of the play which he had felt needed special attention. At last, satisfied with the performance, he dismissed all the students except Ronald, saying he would give him some extra pointers. He asked the others to report to the cafeteria.

"That sounds good to me!" Betty called out. "Come on, Kay!"

They hurried downstairs ahead of the others. Kay and Betty talked about the wigs they were supposed to wear. Betty was sure her head would get so hot she would forget her lines.

"I'm just hoping my headdress won't fall off," said Kay.

It was a happy group which gathered in the cafeteria. Chris had appointed herself a waitress, saying she wanted to pay official honor to the Chinese maiden. She made a mock bow to Kay.

"Take a seat, and I'll bring you some soup," she said, with a sweeping gesture.

"How about waiting on us every day?" Betty asked her.

Chris made a face, and said she was only doing this because it was an important occasion. She wanted to be sure Kay would be rested for her appearance on the stage. Kay and Betty, perplexed, looked at each other. Chris certainly was up to something!

Kay began to eat, but halfway through the bowl of soup, she decided she didn't like the taste of it too much and put down her spoon. Chris came over to remove the bowl.

"Why, Kay," she said, "you aren't eating. You ought to finish the soup. It'll give you lots of pep for tonight."

Kay insisted that she did not want any more of it, so Chris took the bowl away. Instead of bringing the main course to Kay, she went off by herself and started eating her own meal. Betty looked scornfully at her.

"What did I tell you, Kay? I knew the service wouldn't last. Oh, here comes Ronald." He joined them.

Kay ate the rest of the meal, which was delicious.

Then she and Betty went upstairs to meet the woman in charge of makeup for the cast. She seated Kay before a dressing table.

First came makeup cream. This was covered with glowing rouge. Next eye shadow and lipstick were applied. Finally, the woman pencilled on arched eyebrows. Kay looked at herself in the mirror and laughed.

"I hardly recognize myself," she remarked cheerfully, and put on the wig with the fancy headdress.

"You're perfect! Absolutely perfect!" Betty cried in delight.

"Thanks." Kay yawned. "I'm going out for some fresh air. Guess I ate too much. I feel sleepy."

"I'll meet you as soon as I'm made up," said Betty. "See you on the back steps."

Ten minutes later Betty Worth joined her friend. To her astonishment, Kay was seated on the steps, her head resting on her arms. She was sound asleep. Betty nudged her.

"Kay, wake up!"

But Kay did not stir. Frightened, Betty shook her. Kay's eyes opened a tiny bit and she murmured, "Go away."

Betty's brain was in a whirl. This was not a natural sleep! What had happened to Kay?

XVII

Chris Sees A Ghost

Word spread like wildfire that Kay Tracey was ill and would not be able to take her part in the evening's performance. Betty Worth was beside herself. She had asked someone to call Doctor Sage, and, in a few moments, the physician arrived.

In the meantime, Kay had been carried from the school steps to the teachers' lounge. Now she lay on a couch in a deep sleep.

"I can't understand it," Betty told the doctor. "Kay was feeling fine and was very lively until a little while after supper."

After an examination Doctor Sage said he was sure Kay was not coming down with any disease. There was only one answer for her drowsiness: she had eaten or drunk or smelled something that had put her into this state. He asked what Kay had eaten, and Betty described the supper in the cafeteria.

"Has anyone else felt sleepy?" he asked.

Betty went to find out, but returned to say that the other actors and actresses said they felt fine.

"Then I'm inclined to think," said Doctor Sage, "that someone has played a trick by putting a strong sleeping tablet into this girl's food."

He advised that Kay be given a cold shower and strong coffee to drink.

"This should awaken her in time for the performance," he told Betty. "But if not, I'm afraid there's nothing else to be done."

"Why—that would mean we can't give the play!" Betty was close to tears. "Kay has the leading part."

"I'm sorry," the doctor said. "All we can do is hope for the best."

As he left the lounge, the other students crowded around and asked for news of Kay. Doctor Sage repeated what he had told Betty. At once, Chris Eaton sought out Mr. Reynolds.

"I can take Kay's role," she said. "I've been practicing the lines and watching her ever since rehearsals started."

The coach looked at Chris dubiously. But with the situation so desperate, he consented to go to the auditorium with her and review the long speeches.

In the meantime, Betty had sent Jean Striker to make coffee in a hurry. Then she phoned Wendy and asked her to rush over to the school. Wendy, hearing the reason, said she would be there as soon as possible. She called Bill Thomas, whom she dated. He came immediately and drove her to the school.

Wendy ran down to the girls' gym, where Kay had been taken. Then she and Betty took charge. They undressed Kay and pulled a shower cap over her head. By this time the drowsy girl had revived sufficiently from the coffee Betty had forced on her to be able to stay under the shower without assistance. But she kept insisting that all she wanted to do was sleep.

"Kay," Wendy said firmly, "the play is tonight. You have to be in the play!"

"Oh, yes, the play," Kay repeated dully.

But as the cold water struck her full force, Kay opened her eyes wide. She shivered and tried to jump out of the shower, but the Worth twins held her back. Another few seconds under the icy stream and Kay came completely out of her stupor. The doctor's advice had worked!

"What in the world happened to me?" Kay asked, rubbing herself dry with a towel.

Betty told her, and Kay looked worried. "I never felt like this before in my life," she said.

Betty explained Doctor Sage's theory and at once Kay recalled Chris's strange behavior in the cafeteria. Chris had slipped something into the soup! This would account for its peculiar taste.

"Besides," Kay went on, "yesterday at the station I saw Pete hand Chris a small box——"

"Which must have contained whatever put you to sleep," Wendy finished.

"That's a really low thing to do!" Betty cried. "She did it to get your part! Wait till I get hold of Chris. I'll——"

Too angry to go on, Betty started from the shower room to carry out her threat. Kay stopped her and asked her not to bother.

"Chris will be shocked enough to see me," Kay said grimly. "Especially awake!"

She added that since Chris did have her own part, it would be best for the sake of the play if Betty didn't make a scene. Finally, Betty agreed.

The twins helped Kay dress and brought her a robe. Then she hurried to the auditorium. Chris Eaton, already on the stage rehearsing, turned as dead white as if she had seen a ghost. Her voice trailed off to a whisper, and she sagged against the backdrop.

"What's the matter?" Mr. Reynolds asked crossly. "Go on with your part. You said you knew it."

All Chris could do was point at Kay, who was hurrying down the aisle. Mr. Reynolds turned. Seeing her, he jumped up and grasped her hand.

"You're all right, Kay?" he exclaimed, relieved.

"Yes, and I never felt better. That little sleep relaxed me!" Kay raised her voice for Chris's benefit.

"I'm very thankful!" the coach responded warmly. "That will be all, Chris."

He told Kay confidentially that he had been at his wits' end. Chris had learned the lines perfectly but she was little better than a wooden statue on stage. He would have been ashamed to have important visitors see her perform.

"Carmont High drama productions would have lost their good reputation." he said.

Kay did not hear his last sentence! She was staring at the stage setting, which did not look right to her. Suddenly the awful truth dawned on her.

"The Chinese vases, Mr. Reynolds!" she cried out. "They're gone!"

The coach looked, and he, too, was amazed. There was no question about it—the two exquisite, valuable vases were gone!

"Maybe someone just set them aside for safety," Mr. Reynolds said hopefully, as he ran up to the stage.

Kay was already running toward the dressing rooms. She looked thoroughly on the girls' side while Mr. Reynolds searched in the boys'.

When Kay didn't find the vases, she started across the stage to see if Mr. Reynolds had had any better luck. As she came to a tea table which belonged to Mr. Wong, Kay stopped short. The table was not the one from Lotus Gardens! And the chair next to it definitely was a substitute for the original.

"Mr. Reynolds!" Kay cried out. "A thief has been here! The Wongs' things have been stolen!"

XVIII

Curtain Call

Stunned, the coach hurried to Kay's side. He, too, could see that all the small pieces of furniture were indeed substitutions. A larger table, the screen and a silk drapery which Chris had borrowed were still there, but the articles which had been taken were the most valuable.

"But how could it have happened, Kay?" Mr. Reynolds asked.

"It would have been very easy for a thief to get in here and remove the things," said Kay. "The doors aren't locked, and we were all in the cafeteria for nearly an hour. But what puzzles me is why the thief bothered to substitute these other pieces."

The young teacher was very upset. If he called the police, the performance would be held up. A fine impression that would give the foreign visitors!

"Do you have any suggestions?" he asked Kay in despair.

She advised him to notify the police—this was only fair to the Wongs—but perhaps the men would consent not to make an investigation on the stage until the performance was over. As Mr. Reynolds went off, Kay glanced at the wall clock.

"Oh no!" she said. "It's nearly eight o'clock, and people will be arriving any minute! I must get new makeup on."

She dashed off. The makeup artist already had left so Kay asked Wendy and Betty to assist her. While they were working, she told them about the theft of some of the pieces borrowed from the Wongs.

"How awful! What'll Chris and Pete do?" Wendy burst out.

"It's funny Chris didn't notice they were gone," Betty remarked. "She didn't say a word about it when she came back."

"I doubt that she would have seen the change," said Kay. "She was too busy saying my lines!"

Wendy said that Chris had gone into a violent tantrum and no one had seen her since. Suddenly the twin gasped and said that she might have a clue to the identity of the thief!

"As I was coming in here from the street," Wendy remembered, "I noticed a truck at the side entrance. A man was just getting into it. I couldn't say for sure, but he looked something like that Mr. Trexler we met at the auction."

"Really?" Kay asked. "Maybe we should report that to the police, too." She asked Wendy to find Mr. Reynolds and give him this bit of information and to tell them where Trexler's house was located.

She had barely left the room, when one of the girls on the play committee rushed in. "Mr. Reynolds says everybody on stage!" she called out.

"I'll come as fast as I can," Kay said.

Betty helped her into the lovely Chinese embroidered costume and put on the wig with the fancy headdress.

"You look really beautiful," Betty praised her. "Everybody'll love you. And am I glad you're all right! What a mess things would've been with Chris in your part!"

"Thanks, Betty. You look terrific yourself."

The two girls hurried off and through a back entrance of the auditorium to the stage. The audience had just quieted down and the principal was walking onto the stage in front of the curtains.

In the glare of the footlights, he gave a speech of welcome to the visitors and a greeting to all the parents and friends of Carmont High. The auditorium was crowded, and the clapping loud and enthusiastic.

Mr. Reynolds was running nervously back and forth behind the backdrop. "Is everyone ready?" he kept whispering nervously.

Two of the minor characters seated themselves on the stage, and the curtain was pulled back. *The Pagoda Mystery* had started!

It was several minutes before Kay made her entrance. When she did, there were gasps of approval in the audience. Her costume and her dainty gestures were so authentic that it was hard to believe that this was an American girl!

"Kay will be a sensation tonight," whispered Betty, who was standing in the left wing with Ronald. "She's playing her part like a professional!"

"I sure hope I don't ruin any of her scenes," he said. "It's almost time for me to go on, too. Where's my copy of the play? I've already forgotten my first lines."

In desperation Ronald looked for it. He was in a

frenzy of anxiety when Betty gently pushed him out on the stage. For a moment Ronald felt weak in the knees, but Kay gave him a friendly smile which restored his confidence. The forgotten lines came back to him immediately.

As scene after scene progressed smoothly, Ronald became more and more confident of himself. When he would occasionally hesitate for a line, Kay would quietly whisper it to him. The audience meanwhile did not suspect that he had missed a single word.

At the end of the first act it was obvious to everyone that Kay had proven herself a real star. She unconsciously dominated the play.

"You were absolutely wonderful, Kay!" Betty praised, as they met in the girls' dressing room.

"And so were you," Kay replied.

"Well, I didn't forget anything. That was something for me!" Betty chuckled. "But I'll be glad when the play's over."

At length *The Pagoda Mystery* came to an end, but the audience did not leave the auditorium immediately. The clapping went on so long that both Kay and Ronald were obliged to take several bows.

Three bouquets were handed to Kay, and without so much as glancing at the attached cards she smilingly curtsied her appreciation and then escaped to the dressing room.

"Those are gorgeous flowers!" Betty exclaimed. "Why don't you look at the cards?"

Kay was trying to hide the first one, which had Ronald's signature, but Betty snatched it from her hand and read it aloud.

"American Beauty roses, too," she said, smiling.

"This corsage is from Mother and Bill," Kay explained, trying to distract her friend's attention from the roses. "And these——I wonder——"

From a beautiful bunch of fragrant white lilies she removed a tiny card. "Mr. and Mrs. Wong. How sweet!"

"The Wongs didn't come to the play," said Wendy, who had rushed backstage. "Kay, you were superb!"

Wendy went on to say that Mrs. Tracey, Bill and Mrs. Brindell were waiting outside to speak to Kay.

"I'll be there as soon as our pictures have been taken," Kay said.

She and Betty, with the other members of the cast, returned to the stage, and a local photographer snapped picture after picture.

When it was over, Kay noticed Mrs. Brindell standing at the edge of the stage. The woman called to her and offered congratulations. She also said that she would like to take Kay on a little outing in celebration, if she would like to go.

"There's to be an interesting auction over at Long Point tomorrow," she remarked. "You might even find a desk for your cousin. Then I thought in the evening we would go to a play at the Chinese theater there."

Kay was thrilled. This was her chance to find out if Lotus Wong had joined the theatrical company!

XIX

Discovered

"I'd love to go, Mrs. Brindell," Kay said enthusiastically. "Will three-thirty be time enough to start?"

"Yes. I'll pick you up here," the woman told her. "Good-bye and congratulations again on your performance."

"Thank you." Kay turned to speak to her mother and Bill. They each hugged her affectionately, praising her excellent performance. On the way home Kay told them about Mrs. Brindell's invitation, then asked Mrs. Tracey if she could see to having Lotus's beautiful costume dry cleaned.

"I'll thank Mrs. Wong for the flowers before I leave for school tomorrow," she said. "I wonder if she knows yet about the stolen furniture."

"You'd better call the police and find out before you contact Mrs. Wong," Bill advised.

At eight o'clock next morning Kay was on the telephone, asking the Carmont police captain if Sidney Trexler had been located.

"Yes. But we couldn't prefer a charge. We went to

that house you told us about. Mr. Trexler and another man were there. There was no sign of the stolen furniture, and they insisted they had been there all afternoon and evening.

"I'm sorry that the clue seems to have washed out, Miss Tracey," the officer went on. "I guess your friend was mistaken about the person in the truck being Mr. Trexler."

Kay was also told that the Wongs had not been informed yet of the theft, but that the police planned to call them later in the day. The captain asked who the person was that had borrowed the furniture. Kay told them it was Chris Eaton, and felt sure Chris would try to get revenge. Kay decided to put off her phone call to Mrs. Wong until the next day. If she picked up some information that evening at the Chinese theater, Mrs. Wong would want to hear about it.

After Kay had been at school a while, she realized that Chris Eaton was absent. Concerned about the remaining pieces of the Wongs' furnishings, she went to the principal and asked whether Chris planned to return them.

"Mrs. Eaton phoned that Chris was ill and would not be here today," he replied. "I presume she will take care of the furniture tomorrow."

Kay and the Worth twins were more inclined to think that Chris was afraid to come to school. She would avoid the three of them as long as possible. She must have guessed they suspected her of having slipped the pill into Kay's soup.

"School is really pleasant without Chris," Betty remarked as the three hurried through their lunch. She giggled. "Have you noticed how subdued Pete Sparott is?"

Pete was seated by himself eating slowly and looking into space.

"I wonder how long his good behavior will last," said Wendy, and burst out poetically:

> *"Ill wind,*
> *Blow not thy fury nigh!*
> *Disperse!*
> *Cause no tormenting sigh!"*

"To dear old Carmont High!" Betty added.

Kay laughed, then told of her plan to meet Mrs. Brindell after school.

"Lucky you!" commented Betty. "I certainly hope you find Lotus Wong."

"Now that the play is over," said Kay, "I'm going to use every minute I'm not at school for locating that girl."

During the drive to Long Point with Mrs. Brindell, she told the woman a little about Lotus. She pledged her to secrecy, saying Mrs. Wong was afraid to tell her husband that Lotus was missing.

"I won't say a word to anyone." Mrs. Brindell smiled. "This will be an exciting adventure for me.".

Reaching the warehouse where the auction was to be held, she and Kay hurried inside. The sale was already in progress, but Mrs. Brindell said the first things to be auctioned off were small items. She and Kay would look around until the larger pieces were put up.

Kay saw several desks but doubted that her cousin would want any of them in his office. She decided not to bid.

"Isn't this an attractive sofa?" Mrs. Brindell remarked admiringly, pointing to a velvet, brocaded piece. "I believe it's French. Well, we may as well take seats," she suggested. "The auctioneer is about to start the bidding for the large articles."

In a moment he turned his attention to the sofa. "This is a beautiful French antique of unusual value," he announced.

The bidding got off to a fast start, but slackened as the price mounted higher and higher.

"I'll bid $275," Mrs. Brindell offered crisply, as the auctioneer looked questioningly toward her.

A man across the room who had been bidding now shook his head to indicate he would not offer a larger amount. The auctioneer urged his audience, but no one would go higher. Finally he said:

"Do I hear another bid? Going—going——" he paused a moment. "This exquisite French sofa is sold to——"

The auctioneer paused as a man pushed his way through the crowd, crying:

"Just a minute! You can't sell that sofa. It belongs to me!"

Kay turned to look at the man. Sidney Trexler!

"Isn't that the person who interrupted the sale at Lincoln?" Mrs. Brindell asked her in an undertone.

"Yes, it is."

"A rather suspicious coincidence," Mrs. Brindell remarked.

"Very," Kay agreed.

Sidney Trexler was telling the auctioneer that the sofa had been placed in storage by him and that due to press of business he had neglected to keep up regular payments on it. The auctioneer agreed that Trexler might have the sofa if he would pay the amount due for storage.

"Let's protest," Kay proposed.

"No, let him have it," Mrs. Brindell replied. "I don't want to create a scene."

On a hunch Kay followed Trexler to the main desk where he intended to pay the storage fees. He did not notice her, as she tried to overhear what he said. It had occurred to her suddenly that possibly the sofa did not belong to Trexler. By some scheme he had obtained the owner's slip and was taking the piece merely by paying the storage charges.

To her disappointment there was no revealing conversation between him and the clerk. He handed in the necessary papers, which showed the charges of seventy-five dollars and paid them cheerfully. He handed another slip to the clerk, saying he would like the sofa delivered to that address.

Kay wanted to find out more and wondered if she should speak to the clerk. She could not think of any good pretext to do so, however. As she tried to figure one out, Mrs. Brindell walked back to join her.

"There isn't anything else here I want to bid on," she told Kay. "Suppose we have dinner and then go to the theater."

She and Kay left the warehouse and walked up the street. Reaching a Chinese restaurant, Mrs. Brindell suggested they go in.

"I thought we'd make an entire Chinese evening of it," she said, smiling.

"That'll be fun," Kay responded, holding the door open for the woman.

The oriental restaurant was attractively furnished and several Chinese waitresses stood about. Since it was early, there were few diners in the place. Mrs. Brindell and Kay were shown to a table about halfway down the room, and large menu cards were offered to them by the headwaiter.

"Oh," said Kay, glancing at hers. "These dishes are a real puzzle to me. Please, Mrs. Brindell, would you order for me?"

Mrs. Brindell nodded and began studying the card. Meanwhile, Kay's eyes roamed about the room. The furnishings and pictures were unusual, and she presumed they had been imported.

Kay's attention was distracted by the opening of swinging doors at the rear of the restaurant. A Chinese waitress appeared and stood near an empty table. Suddenly Kay grasped her companion's hand.

"Mrs. Brindell," she said excitedly, "that waitress back there—I believe she's Lotus Wong!"

"Are you sure?"

Kay quickly opened her bag and took out the picture which the girl's mother had given her. Mrs. Brindell glanced at the photograph, then at the waitress.

"I believe you're right, Kay," she exclaimed. "Let's take that table down there. It's a bit drafty here anyway."

The two got up and walked toward the rear. The Chinese girl smiled at the two as they seated themselves. Kay studied her face intently. She was absolutely certain this was Lotus Wong!

Before Kay could ask her, one of the diners on the other side of the room dropped a dish. The clatter caused a momentary distraction, as everyone looked in that direction.

To Kay's complete surprise, the person responsible for the accident was Cara Noma! As the three gazed at her, the woman began to make queer hypnotic motions with her hands.

Snakelike, she got up from her chair and moved menacingly toward them!

XX

A Painted Dragon

Was Cara Noma trying to spoil Kay's plans?

Putting her hand on the Chinese waitress's shoulder, she turned her around away from the medium's gaze. Smiling at the girl disarmingly, Kay said:

"You're Lotus Wong, aren't you?"

Taken unaware, the pretty girl seemed about to say yes, then fear seized her.

"No, no! You are mistaken!" she cried.

In a flash she ran through the swinging doors to the kitchen.

By this time Cara Noma had reached Kay and Mrs. Brindell. "Why are you here?" she demanded of Kay.

Mrs. Brindell looked puzzled and alarmed. Kay introduced the two women. Then on a sudden hunch that the medium would cause Lotus Wong more trouble, Kay got up and went through the swinging doors also.

Cara Noma was at her heels. "You meddler!" she cried. "Get out of here!"

The Chinese cooks and waitresses looked up startled. Lotus Wong was not in sight. Paying no attention to the medium, Kay asked one of the other girls where Lotus had gone.

"There is no one by that name here," was the reply.

"I mean the girl who just ran into the kitchen."

"Oh, that's Lily Sen."

This was all Kay needed. She was sure Lotus was using her mother's maiden name. Learning that Lotus had left by the rear door, Kay went after her. So did Cara Noma.

Reaching an alleyway leading to the street, the medium caught up to Kay and pushed her violently to the pavement. By the time Kay could get up and reach the street, the medium was far down the block. She turned the corner swiftly.

Kay ran after her, but before she could overtake the woman, the medium had jumped into a car and had started off. Kay was sure someone was seated alongside her. Lotus Wong probably!

"And I was so close to finding out something!" Kay thought in vexation.

Returning to the restaurant through the front door, Kay asked for the manager. She explained to him that the waitress calling herself Lily Sen had run away from home. Her mother was distracted, and hoped Kay might find her. Did he know where the girl lived?

The man looked through his records and finally said, "Miss Sen's address is in care of the Chinese theater here." He smiled apologetically. "The Orient pays very poorly, so the actors and actresses must take other jobs to earn a living."

"I see," said Kay. "I'm going there tonight. No doubt I'll see Miss Sen."

She returned to Mrs. Brindell and told her what had happened.

"I doubt Lotus Wong will go to the theater tonight," the woman said.

Kay agreed. "There's a good chance Cara Noma may take her away. If I could only find out where Lotus has been living, I might stop her."

"Why don't you call the Orient and inquire?" Mrs. Brindell suggested.

Kay went to a phone booth and dialed the number. But there was no answer. Evidently the theater did not open until later.

When a waitress came to take her order, Kay asked her if she would mind inquiring among the employees in the restaurant if anyone knew where Lily Sen lived.

The answer was a discouraging one. The girl had kept very much to herself and not divulged anything of her private life to the other workers.

Kay sighed in disappointment. After they had finished eating, she called the theater again. This time there was an answer. Kay was told that Lily Sen had phoned she would not be able to appear that evening—in fact, she was not returning to the Orient.

"Could you give me her address?" Kay inquired.

Obtaining it, she asked Mrs. Brindell if they could drive over there before going to the Orient. Mrs. Brindell agreed, but as Kay suspected, Lily Sen had packed her clothes quickly and left the boardinghouse.

"Now I'll have to start my search all over again," Kay frowned.

During the evening she could hardly keep her mind on the Chinese play. The substitute who had taken Lotus Wong's place was very poor, and the performance was not up to expectations. As Kay and Mrs. Brindell walked from the theater, Mrs. Brindell whispered:

"I enjoyed the play last night much more."

"I did too," Kay smiled.

Since she had no new lead to the whereabouts of Lotus Wong, Kay decided not to call on the girl's mother yet. But when she noticed the next afternoon that the Chinese costume she had borrowed from Mrs. Wong had been returned from the cleaner's, she made up her mind to visit Lotus Gardens.

Mrs. Tracey went with her. They spent a delightful hour with Mrs. Wong, who seemed to have divorced herself completely from Cara Noma's influence.

Furthermore, Mrs. Wong said she had had a note from her daughter. Lotus had apologized for not having been in touch with her mother, but said she had had to make a trip away from college in connection with her work. Lotus would not return for some time, but would write to her mother again.

"Then you don't want me to search for Lotus any more?" Kay asked.

"Lily Wong not sure," she replied. "One time news seem good. Next minute news very bad."

Mrs. Wong seemed to be struggling with a thought she was not sure should be divulged to Kay. Kay wondered if it concerned Cara Noma, but thought it best not to mention the medium's name. When the pause became embarrassing, she said:

"Mrs. Wong, does your husband own a boat?"

"Not now," Mrs. Wong replied. "Husband have fine boat year ago. He sell."

"Was it a large one?" Kay asked.

"You call yacht?" Mrs. Wong answered. She

smiled. "Husband paint big dragon on deck. Lotus say she afraid of dragon."

"Was that why Mr. Wong sold the boat?"

"Lily Wong not know. Husband not discuss business with wife."

Mrs. Tracey got up to leave. As she did, they heard the front door slam. A moment later Mr. Wong walked into the room.

"Good afternoon, Miss Tracey," he said, smiling.

Kay introduced her mother, and Mr. Wong bowed low.

"I am very happy to meet you, Mrs. Tracey," he remarked. "You have a fine, very bright daughter."

He insisted that they stay and have a bowl of tea with him. While they were drinking the tea, Mr. Wong, who seemed to be unusually cheerful, said he was making a wedding gift for his daughter. It would be both unusual and beautiful.

"It will contain the finest green cameo in the world. The cameo is in this cabinet," he said, touching the piece of furniture.

Mrs. Wong gasped. Her husband looked at her angrily.

Kay was surprised. Since the time the cameo had been snatched away from her by a man's hand reaching through the secret panel, not one word had been said about it by the Wongs. Evidently Mr. Wong had been responsible, and had returned the cameo to its hiding place.

"Perhaps, Mrs. Tracey, you would like to see the green cameo?" Mr. Wong asked her.

Mrs. Tracey was not especially anxious to, but she said yes, nevertheless. Mr. Wong opened the front door of the cabinet, reached inside, and clicked the secret spring.

The next moment a strange look came over his face. Frantically he stretched out his arm and felt around. Then he cried out:

"The green cameo is gone!"

The others stared in horror as the man's face became livid. He beat upon his chest, crying out angrily in Chinese. Finally he pointed a finger at Kay.

"You are the thief!" he snarled.

XXI

The Hideout

———————————◆———————————

"No! No! I'm not a thief!" Kay cried.

Mrs. Tracey stepped between her daughter and the angry Mr. Wong. Her eyes flashing, she spoke sternly.

"Mr. Wong, I think your anger has gotten the better of you. If you will calm yourself, you will realize that my daughter knows nothing about this missing green cameo."

As Mr. Wong continued to glare at Kay, Mrs. Wong arose from her chair, and hurried toward her husband. Reaching out her hands in supplication, she spoke to him in Chinese. The words seemed to have an electric effect upon him.

In an instant his whole demeanor had changed. He apologized profusely to Kay and her mother, explaining that the loss of the green cameo was a great blow to him. While he was not superstitious about it like his wife was, he did not want to lose the piece. It was too valuable.

"Also, I shall not be able to make a beautiful wedding gift for my daughter without it," he said.

Mrs. Wong looked anxiously at Kay, as if to ask that the girl not say anything about Lotus. Kay had no intention of doing so, but she suggested to Mr. Wong that he get in touch with the police.

Mr. Wong opposed this advice vehemently. He said he already had a pretty good idea who had stolen the green cameo. If they would please excuse him now, he would try to find the guilty person.

After he left, Kay asked his wife if she had any idea who the suspect might be. Mrs. Wong said no, and she herself did not suspect anyone. Kay and her mother said good-bye, adding that they hoped the green cameo would soon be returned.

When they were in the car driving toward Brantwood, Kay confided that she had her own theory about who had taken the cameo.

"You have? Who?"

"Cara Noma!" Kay replied.

"Well, that's a surprise," remarked Mrs. Tracey, "I thought you were going to say it was Chang."

Kay said that she was certain of his loyalty to the Wongs. She did not know that he was to be trusted outside the family, but she doubted that he would actually steal anything from his employers.

"Tomorrow I'm going to pay a visit to Cara Noma," Kay announced. "And I'll take Betty and Wendy with me."

"You mean you're going to Lincoln?" her mother asked. "But if Cara Noma suspects you, don't you think she has moved out long since?"

Kay laid an affectionate hand on her mother's arm.

"Mother dear, you're a good detective yourself!" she said, laughing.

Kay went on to say that even if the trip drew a blank, she had another plan up her sleeve. She was going out to Trexler's house and talk to him if he were there. If not, perhaps she could pick up a clue from someone else who might be at his place.

"Do be careful, dear," her mother cautioned, and Kay promised to keep out of danger.

When she told Betty and Wendy the next day about her plan, Wendy was especially eager to go. She had been annoyed that the police had not believed her identification of Trexler.

"I'm sure he was the one in front of school the evening the furniture was stolen," she declared.

"Maybe he keeps his stuff some other place," Betty suggested.

Kay agreed with this theory. It was not likely that if Trexler were bringing a bride to the new home, he would keep stolen goods there, least of all, something from the Wong home!

"Do you still believe what Chris said—that Trexler's engaged to Lotus Wong?" Wendy asked.

Kay shrugged. Chris had seemed positive at the time, but recent events had proved Chris wasn't very reliable. Even if Chris were wrong, however, the situation did not help Lotus Wong. She was still destined, against her will, to marry a man named Foochow!

"I honestly can't see where Cara Noma fits into the picture," Betty spoke up. "If the Wongs are giving her money——"

"That's just the point," said Kay. "I'm sure Mrs. Wong is no longer under the medium's influence, so Cara Noma is probably losing a lot of income."

"And had to steal the green cameo to make up the difference." Betty giggled.

They were not too surprised when they reached Lincoln that afternoon and pulled up in front of Cara Noma's place to discover a *for rent* sign in the window. Kay made inquiries in a neighboring store but learned nothing to help find Cara Noma.

"I wonder if Mr. Wong is having any better luck than we are," Kay mused, as they got into the car again and set off for Sidney Trexler's small house on the outskirts of town.

Another disappointment awaited them there. No one answered the bell, and nothing about the place indicated that anyone was at home. The girls looked through the windows and saw that the house was very attractively decorated.

"It looks as though Mr. Trexler has the place ready for his bride," commented Betty.

They had started down the lane from the house and just reached the main road, when they saw a rural mail carrier driving toward them in a mud-spattered car.

"Let's wait a minute and see if he stops here," Kay suggested on a sudden impulse.

She was excited when the postman halted in front of the metal box bearing Trexler's name.

"Good afternoon," Kay said to the old man. "We came to see Mr. Trexler, but he's not at home. Have you any idea where we might find him?"

"Maybe over at Bartley," the mailman replied. "That's where he spends most of his time."

"You mean he's in business there?" Kay asked.

"I guess so. Once he asked me to forward some mail to a place on Elm Street," the man answered.

Kay's heart was pounding. Here was a clue at last!

"You don't remember the number, do you?" she asked innocently.

"Can't say that I do," the postman replied. "But I think it was on the corner of Bridge and Elm."

"Thank you so much," said Kay gratefully.

"You're welcome," he said.

As they drove off, Kay asked her friends if they were game to go on to Bartley and continue sleuthing.

"You bet we are!" Betty answered for the twins.

Fortunately for the young detectives, there was only one business building at Elm and Bridge streets. One corner was vacant and on the other two were apartment houses.

Kay squeezed her car into a small parking space between two automobiles. Before getting out, they surveyed the one story office building. It appeared to be deserted. A large glass window was plastered with signs and posters, and the interior was empty.

"This can't be the place," Wendy remarked.

"It's just exactly the kind of place that Trexler would use if he's up to something funny," Kay objected.

"But there's nothing inside."

"He might be using the basement."

The three of them circled the building. The cellar windows were boarded up, giving the impression that no one used the place. Kay found a door leading from the alleyway driveway into the main floor of the building. She tried it and was surprised to find the door unlocked.

"Let's go in and look around," she suggested.

"We might get arrested for trespassing," Wendy said nervously. But when Kay and Betty entered, she followed.

Kay found a door which apparently led to the basement. Opening it, she heard sounds below.

"Something's going on here. Let's look!"

Betty and Wendy crept down the stairs behind Kay. Though the basement was not well lighted, they could see furniture stacked along the walls.

"There's that French sofa I told you about," Kay whispered, pointing.

"What is this place?" Wendy asked, as they reached the bottom step. "A private warehouse?"

"Sh!" Betty warned. "What's that?"

From a distance the girls could hear a faint hammering. They moved silently in its direction.

A streak of light shone from under a door. Kay opened it softly and looked down a short circular staircase into a subbasement.

A small force of workmen were busy at benches. Blueprints and sketches were spread out before them. Some of the men were occupied at lathes, others were varnishing and painting furniture.

"Why is all this so secret?" Wendy whispered.

"I'd say Mr. Trexler copies fine old pieces and sells them as antiques," Kay guessed.

As the trio backed cautiously up the stairs, they became aware of voices down a corridor. Tiptoeing along, they came to an office. Their eyes widened as they saw the occupants of the room—Sidney Trexler, and a young woman who was typing.

But Kay's eyes were drawn to something of even more interest. Neatly stacked on a table were a whole pile of jewelry boxes that looked just like Mr. Wong's. And on Trexler's desk was Lotus Wong's box which he had purchased at the Lincoln auction! Was he copying this to sell at some exorbitant price?

"It's getting late," the man said to the stenographer a moment later. "Why doesn't that guy come? He sure takes his own sweet time," Trexler added crossly.

"Why can't Mr. Foochow pack Mr. Wong's jewelry boxes and send them himself?" the girl asked.

Kay's heart was beating like a drum. Jewelry boxes! Wong! Foochow! Was this the man Lotus's father expected her to marry?

"Something very strange is going on," she thought.

Wendy grabbed Kay's arm and whispered, "Let's get out of here! We'll be caught!"

But there was no time. She had barely finished speaking when they heard footsteps on the stairs. They moved swiftly behind a stack of cartons and waited.

XXII

Foochow's Trick

As Kay and the twins watched tensely, a heavyset Chinese man appeared.

His face was cruel and sullen, and he strode into Trexler's office briskly. "You know the rule," he snapped. "I must have peace and quiet while I arrange the boxes for shipment. You will step outside while I work."

"Certainly, Mr. Foochow," was Trexler's response.

He and his secretary got up quickly from their chairs and went into the hall. Foochow watched them until they disappeared down the stairway to the workroom.

Kay could hardly restrain a cry as she realized that before her very eyes was the man who intended to marry Lotus Wong. Foochow himself!

"Ugh! I certainly wouldn't want him for a husband," she thought.

To the girls' disappointment he turned his back, so that they could not see what he was doing. They guessed, however, from his motions, that he was inserting something into the boxes. Whatever the article was he had not wanted the others to see it. Taking a list from his pocket, he laid it on top of the boxes and left the room.

"Where are you going, Kay?" cried Wendy, as the man disappeared up the steps and her friend slid from behind the cartons.

Kay dashed into the office. Quickly she read a couple of names on the list, then flew back to her hiding place.

"The boxes are going to Chinese people in Seattle and Detroit," she said.

"Sh!" Betty warned. "Trexler and the girl are coming back!"

The couple were talking animatedly. "I just can't understand that guy," the secretary said as they entered the office. "You know what I think! That there's a secret compartment in these boxes and he slipped something into them."

Trexler picked up one of the boxes and examined it carefully. He pushed, pulled and shook it. If there were a secret drawer, he could not find the combination. At last he shook his head, saying he did not believe the girl was right about any secret.

Then he did a most surprising thing. He walked over and kissed her.

"Sylvia, my dear," he said, "after we're married, don't fool me like that."

Behind the carton the three girls looked at one another. So this was Trexler's fiancée, not Lotus Wong!

"Sylvia," he said, "how about our going to a Chinese restaurant for supper? I'm just in the mood."

"You're not going to ask me to dress up like a Chinese Princess the way I did at the college masquerade, are you?" she teased.

Kay and the twins could hardly keep from laughing out loud. Trexler had given Chris Eaton a great line—saying he was engaged to a Chinese Princess!

The couple left the building, and the three girls followed when the way seemed clear. Reaching the street, they looked around carefully so the two would not spot them. Then they crossed the street to their car.

"I wonder where Mr. Foochow went," said Kay. "I wish I could find out more about him."

She did not like his looks, or his actions. "I bet his business methods are on the shady side."

"What do you think he was putting into those boxes?" Betty asked her.

"I have no idea," Kay replied. "I almost wish I had tried to find the secret compartment."

By the gleam in her eye, Betty and Wendy knew something was up.

"You're not going back into that building are you?" cried Wendy anxiously.

Kay smiled. "No. Don't worry."

"Why do you suppose Foochow didn't want Trexler to know what he was placing in the boxes?" Betty asked. "Even if Mr. Trexler isn't too honest about what he does with furniture, I don't believe he's involved with Mr. Foochow, do you, Kay?"

"No. Probably Mr. Foochow just uses him to pack those jewelry boxes and ship them."

Kay paused, then added, "I wonder if there's some connection with Mr. Wong. Maybe those boxes aren't imitations after all, and there's more to Lotus's marriage than we think."

"You mean that it might be just a marriage of convenience?" Wendy asked, and started to burst into a poem on the subject, when Kay grabbed her arm.

"Look!" she cried. "There's Mr. Foochow! Coming out of that door!"

A tall man who was not an Oriental followed him from a tobacco shop. They walked down the street together.

"Come on!" Kay urged. "Maybe we can find out something!"

Without running, they made good time down the street. In a few moments they had gotten near Mr. Foochow and his friend. The men stopped near a car, and went on with their conversation.

Kay deliberately dropped her bag with such force that the contents spilled out. Betty and Wendy stooped to help her pick them up.

The men paid no attention. They didn't even lower their voices and it was easy for the girls to hear every word they were saying.

"You're pulling out Monday night, right?" the American asked.

"Yes, and don't be late," Foochow replied.

The other man chuckled. "Don't worry. The *Wingate* won't sail without me!"

"We pull anchor at nine o'clock sharp," Foochow told him. "By then all the new work will be delivered. There'll be no reason for hanging around."

"If you should sail before nine o'clock," the other man said, "where will you dock, so I can find you?"

Foochow's beady eyes became slits. "Foochow's word is law," he reminded him. "When I say we pull away from Big Cove at nine o'clock, I mean nine o'clock!"

With this cutting remark, he opened the car door

and slid over into the driver's seat. He did not say good-bye or look at the other man as he pulled away from the curb. By this time Kay and the twins had finished scooping up the various articles from Kay's bag.

Kay smiled. Now the mystery was beginning to take shape. She was sure that the boat called the *Wingate* had belonged to Mr. Wong. It was just the clue she needed!

"You think Lotus may be living on the boat?" asked Wendy.

"No, not that. But I do believe something sinister is going on aboard the *Wingate*. I'm sure Lotus is innocent, but I'm not so sure about her father—or Cara Noma."

"Kay, I'll bet that brain of yours is trying to figure out how you can get on the *Wingate* and find out what's happening," said Wendy.

Kay chuckled. "You guessed it. And I've just figured out how I can do it. I'll dress as a boy and go aboard!"

XXIII

Jigsaw Clues

"That's too dangerous!" cried Wendy.

Kay asked her and Betty not to worry. She would be careful.

"I bet your mother wouldn't let you go if she knew," Wendy told her. "Mystery or no mystery, I'd stay away from that mean-looking Foochow."

"Well, just to please you," said Kay, "I'll ask my mother. If she doesn't want me to go, okay."

A little later Kay laughed out loud when she thought of her promise to Wendy. On reaching home, she had found that both her mother and Bill had gone away. There was a note on the table for Kay, saying an accident had occurred to a relative in a distant city. They had rushed off to help. Would Kay please go over and spend a couple of days with Betty and Wendy until Mrs. Tracey returned?

Kay picked up the phone and dialed her friends'

home. "Guess you'll have to play mother to a little boy," she said, giggling, and explained that she would be over to spend the night.

"Wonderful," replied Betty, who answered the phone. "I'll pick you up in a few minutes."

Mrs. Worth was told Kay's plan for Monday evening. She was not sure about giving permission, and asked them to call some of their male friends since she and her husband could not go. But Ronald and the twins' friends were going to be in a big game and had promised the coach they would go to bed early.

Kay finally talked Mrs. Worth into letting her make the trip, with the promise that Kay would not be far from Wendy and Betty at any time.

As soon as school closed on Monday, the three went to a department store in Carmont to buy some boys' clothes for Kay. Then they set out for Big Cove.

It was a tedious ride and it was nearly suppertime when the girls reached the town. Betty, who was driving, headed for the waterfront. They drove almost the full length without seeing the *Wingate*.

"It looks as if we've come on a wild-goose chase," Wendy remarked.

"Maybe the boat sailed ahead of time," Betty added.

Kay said nothing, and they drove on. Finally only one pier was left. There was a good-sized building on it which hid any boat that might be docked.

"I'll get out and run up to see if the *Wingate*'s here," said Kay, opening the car door.

She ran down the pier, but returned in a few seconds. Her eyes were shining.

"The boat's here!" she said excitedly.

"When are you going aboard?" Wendy asked.

Kay said that she would not dare try her stunt until

after dark. "Around eight o'clock," she replied.

"Then we have two hours to wait," Betty remarked. "Are we going to spend all that time eating supper?"

"I have another idea," said Kay. "Let's hunt for Cara Noma."

The twins wanted to know what had put this farfetched idea in Kay's head.

"That's simple," Kay laughed. "Cara Noma had to leave Lincoln in a hurry. If she's mixed up in this mystery, it would be natural for her to come here."

"That sounds reasonable," Betty agreed. "Sailors often go to fortune-tellers. Let's ask that old man over there if he knows her."

The girls walked over to him, and Kay asked if there were any fortune-tellers in town. The old man smiled, saying there were several.

"Some are good, some not so good," he replied. "I heard just yesterday that there's a new one in town. She hypnotizes people before she tells their fortunes."

The girls could hardly contain their excitement. This certainly sounded like Cara Noma!

"What's this new woman's name?" Kay asked.

"I think they call her Bella Clara," the sailor replied. "You can find her place up the street a couple of blocks. You can't miss it."

They thanked him and hurried back to their car. They drove the two blocks and began looking for the medium's place of business. They soon saw a sign in the window. It was wedged in between two other stores with apartments over them.

"Are you going in?" Wendy asked Kay.

"I guess I'd better not," she replied. "But let's see if we can catch a glimpse of Bella Clara."

This proved to be easy, for as a client emerged

from the establishment, the medium came to the door with her. She was Cara Noma!

After the woman had gone back inside, Kay hopped out of the car and walked into the adjoining store. It was a delicatessen. A pleasant faced woman stood behind the counter. Kay bought a box of cookies and engaged her in conversation. Presently Kay said:

"I see a fortune-teller has come next door. Have you been in yet?"

"No, not yet," the woman answered, "but I hear she's good."

"Does she live around here?" Kay asked.

"Oh yes. She lives upstairs. Funny thing, she has a Chinese girl living with her."

Kay could hardly keep from showing her excitement. She asked if the girl helped Bella Clara.

"No, she works as a waitress in the Chinese restaurant here," the woman replied.

"Thank you," said Kay, and returned to the car.

Betty and Wendy were astounded to hear the news. The detectives were certainly in luck!

"Where's the restaurant?" Betty inquired.

Kay asked a passerby and was directed to a spot down the street.

"I'm not going to make the mistake I did last time I saw Lotus Wong," said Kay. "I'll have a note ready to be delivered to her."

She pulled a notebook from her handbag and wrote:

"Dear Lotus Wong: Please don't run away. We are friends and have just about proved that Mr. Foochow is not honest. I need your help. Kay Tracey."

Kay folded the note and put it into her pocket. "Even if Lotus does run away from the restaurant," she said, "this time I know where to find her."

She asked Betty and Wendy to walk in front of her so that if Lotus Wong were near the door, she would not notice Kay. They sat down at a table by the door and Kay rested her head in her hands, trying to cover as much of her face as possible. But she searched the restaurant thoroughly for Lotus.

"There she is!" whispered Kay tensely a moment later. "The one near that stairway."

She asked Wendy to deliver the note, then come back and sit down. Wendy did it, and the three girls waited to see what effect the message would have on Lotus Wong.

Lotus read the note several times, then looked up. Finally she walked toward them.

The ruse had worked!

"I do not know exactly what you mean," she said. "Would you mind telling me more about it?"

"You *are* Lotus Wong?" Kay asked her.

"Yes, I am, and I admit I did run away from home. You must know that Mr. Foochow is the reason."

"I guessed as much," said Kay.

As quickly as she could, Kay told the story of the mystery and how she had become involved in it.

"I'm sorry to have hurt my mother," the girl said, "but I just can't marry Mr. Foochow."

Kay told of her plans to board the *Wingate* secretly that night and asked Lotus if she would come with them. Lotus seemed frightened at the thought but finally consented.

"Does the *Wingate* belong to your father?" Kay asked her.

Lotus shook her head, saying that her father's boat had been called the *Green Cameo*. As she served the visitors their supper they all talked of the mystery and Kay's chances of learning whether something sinister was going on aboard the *Wingate*. Finally Kay broached the subject of Cara Noma.

"I never should have listened to that woman," Lotus confided. "She is the one who advised me to run away to avoid marrying Mr. Foochow. I shouldn't admit it, but Cara Noma mesmerizes me."

"I hope she won't mesmerize you any more," said Kay. "I'm sure she's not honest and we suspect she has stolen the green cameo from your parents."

Instead of looking alarmed at this news, Lotus Wong seemed pleased. She said the presence of the cameo in the house had made her mother unhappy for many years. It had also caused great unhappiness between her and Mr. Wong because he was not superstitious about it the way her mother was.

"I know it's valuable," said Lotus, "but I almost wish it won't be found."

At seven-thirty Kay said they would leave and return for Lotus in half an hour. She told her about having the boys' clothes in the car and Lotus smiled. Kay said she would drive out of town a little and put them on.

After she and the twins left the restaurant, Kay said she was going to the police station and report Cara Noma. The desk sergeant listened attentively to Kay's story, saying the police certainly would investigate.

"If this medium has the green cameo," the sergeant said, "we'll find it!"

Kay thanked him and left the station house. She and her friends drove a mile out of town and Kay put on her costume for the evening. It consisted of corduroy slacks, a jacket and sneakers. The twins said that she looked really cute with her hair tucked up under a cap.

It was dark by the time they picked up Lotus and

drove to the pier. Kay asked them all to wait in the car, then stepped out.

"If I don't return in forty minutes, get the police," she instructed.

"You bet we will," Betty assured her.

Stealthily Kay walked to the waterfront and stood in hiding several minutes watching the *Wingate*. She glanced up and down the deserted shore, then noiselessly darted up the gangplank.

Reaching the deck, she froze in her tracks. Someone was coming! Huddling in the shadow of a smokestack, the girl listened intently.

"Who's there?" a voice thundered.

XXIV

An Iron Grip

Kay crouched motionless in the shadow of the smokestack. From an open hatchway a man cautiously emerged. He looked carefully up and down the deck but didn't see Kay.

"I was sure I heard someone," he muttered.

The man made a complete tour of the deck, passing within a few feet of where Kay stood. He could have reached out and touched her if he had known she was there!

Finally the man went below. After waiting several minutes to make certain he would not return, Kay crept from her hiding place. It struck her as odd that the deck was unguarded. From the hold of the vessel she could hear voices and a strange rumbling noise.

"I wonder what that sound can be?" Kay thought. "It must be machinery."

Quietly she stole down the companionway. It was

dark below, but far ahead of her she could see the faint gleam of lights. The noise of moving machines was clearer now.

Kay became aware of a strange odor. What was it? Ink! Fresh ink! The clattering, rumbling noise must be coming from a printing press!

Kay stole swiftly along the dark corridor toward the workroom. Coming to a door which was slightly ajar, she cautiously peered in.

The room held a compact, complete printing unit. Three men were working at the press and benches, making and stacking counterfeit ten dollar bills!

"So this is what Mr. Foochow does!" Kay thought grimly. "He slips counterfeit money into those jewel boxes and ships them to other Chinese!

"I wonder if the bills Mrs. Worth got in San Francisco came from here?" Kay wondered. "I wish I could find out."

An opportunity came a moment later. A workman picked up a stack of bills and set them on the floor near the door, face down. Kay peered at the picture of the old car. It was blurry!

"I'd better report this to the Big Cove police!" she decided.

But just then the men began to talk again. She would wait. They might mention the names of those in the counterfeit gang.

"I'll be glad when we lift anchor," one of the Americans said. "We can't fool those Secret Service men forever."

"Yeah, but try to change Foochow's mind," the other said. "He'll have Cara Noma puttin' a curse on you."

Cara Noma! Was she involved in the racket? Kay

instantly thought of the counterfeit bill the woman had dropped at the Wong estate. Had she been paid with it by Foochow, or was she distributing them also?

As the men stopped speaking, Kay decided to leave. But before she could turn, a powerful hand gripped her shoulder firmly.

"You sneak!" a voice hissed in her ear.

Kay struggled to free herself, but the leering Oriental man who had caught her held her with a very strong grip. He dragged her into the room where the press was running.

"A spy," he announced. "There may be others aboard. Search the boat."

Instantly the men abandoned their work and the press was turned off. Kay had never seen so many cruel, evil faces in one place before. What were the counterfeiters going to do with her?

"Take the boy on deck," a voice ordered.

The command came as a shock to Kay. A boy! For the moment she had forgotten her disguise. Should she reveal her identity and beg for mercy? No, she would wait and hope for an opportunity to escape.

Kay was jerked roughly up the companionway to the open deck, and the men gathered about her.

"How did you get aboard?" one of them demanded harshly.

"I just walked up the gangplank," Kay replied, disguising her voice. "I didn't mean any harm."

"Oh yeah?" another shouted furiously. "I bet somebody sent you."

Two men had already searched the *Wingate*. Although they had found no one, they were unwilling to believe Kay's claim that she had boarded the vessel without companions.

"Hitch the boy to a yardarm and dip him in the drink," one of the sailors advised with a leer. "That ought to loosen his tongue!"

"I've told you the truth," Kay said frantically. She fought to keep back the tears. Her arm was being painfully twisted.

"Hold there!" a voice called sharply.

"It's the big boss himself," one of the men muttered.

All of them stood at attention except the sailor who was holding Kay firmly by the arms. In the dim light Foochow regarded Kay with an intense scrutiny that sent chills racing up and down her back.

"What are you doing to this boy?" he demanded.

"We caught him spying below decks, sir."

"A spy, eh? He saw our work?"

"He saw everything. When we caught him he was looking in the door of the press room."

Foochow turned to face Kay again. His evil expression told her more plainly than words could that she could expect no mercy.

"Are you a government agent?" he questioned harshly.

Kay shook her head.

"I think the boy is lying," he said to his workers. "Government men sent him here."

"No!" Kay denied, keeping her face averted.

Should she reveal her true identity? It might only make the situation worse by involving her family and friends. She doubted that he would show her any leniency merely because she was a girl.

"We sail at once!" Foochow said. Leering at Kay, he added evenly, "You will spend the rest of your life on shipboard as my guest!"

He gave terse orders and the sailors rushed to carry

them out. The gangplank was quickly raised, and the powerful gasoline engines vibrated through the ship.

Kay's heart sank. Her plan had failed and she was a prisoner. The forty minutes were not yet up. She could expect no help from her friends or the police.

The harassed girl could see the shoreline gradually receding. If only she were not guarded it would be a simple matter to jump overboard and swim to safety. Soon that would be impossible.

In the excitement of getting off, Foochow seemingly had lost interest in Kay, but he had not forgotten her. When the vessel was well under way he walked over toward where she stood, carefully watched.

At this very instant Kay looked down and spied the faint outline of a large dragon painted on the deck. So this had been Mr. Wong's boat!

"Mr. Foochow," she said bravely, "don't think you can get away with this. Mr. Wong and his daughter know what's going on here. The police are on your trail right now!"

The man stopped short. Taken off guard, he said, "The police!"

Then a cunning look came into his eyes. "Maybe you are right, but by the time they arrive all the evidence will be gone. And you will not be here as a witness!"

The sinister meaning behind Foochow's words was not immediately clear to Kay. Even when he ordered two guards to bind her hands and feet with stout ropes she did not guess her captors' intentions.

But as they dragged her across the deck toward the railing, the terrible truth suddenly dawned on her.

She was to be thrown overboard to drown!

XXV

Daring Strategy

Drowning! Kay was stunned.

Although she was an excellent swimmer, Kay knew she didn't have a chance of reaching shore with both her hands and feet tied.

"Wait!" Kay cried frantically. "Don't throw me overboard! I'll tell you more!"

Her pleas fell on deaf ears. As the guards lifted her, she struggled desperately and turned an appealing face to Foochow who was watching the scene, unmoved.

In her tussle with the guards Kay's cap was pulled from her head. Her hair came tumbling down in a shining cloud.

"A girl!" Foochow cried out. "Wait!" he ordered them. "Maybe we make big mistake."

He stared at Kay's clothing. "Who are you?" he asked.

"Kay Tracey from Brantwood. I know the Wongs.

Lotus ran away from home and her mother asked me to
find her. That's all."

Foochow ordered the boat stopped. Kay wondered wildly if he was going to turn back. But her hopes
were soon dashed.

"We will anchor here until I find out more of this
story," Foochow said. "Miss Tracey, you said Lotus had
run away from home. What do you mean?"

Wisely Kay mentioned nothing about the real
reason for Lotus having left. She said that the girl had a
beautiful voice and wanted to go on the stage. Feeling
that her father would not let her do this, she had run
away and joined a Chinese troupe.

"Where is Lotus now?" Foochow asked her.

Kay's courage returned. She decided to bargain
with the man. "If I tell you, will you let me go?" she
asked.

"I'll see about that," the Chinese replied.

Kay shrugged. "You will never find her if I don't
tell you where she is," she said boldly.

Foochow was undecided what to do. He paced
nervously back and forth across the deck, gazing
toward the distant lights along the shore. Finally he
came back to Kay.

"Untie her, men!" he said. "Lower a boat for me.
Miss Tracey will stay here until I return. I will check her
story."

While Kay's ropes were being removed, Foochow
asked where he could find Lotus Wong.

"Suppose you take me with you and I'll lead you to
her," Kay suggested.

Foochow said he would not do this. His men
would verify that he always kept his word. If he found
Kay's story to be true, he would release her. After all,
with the evidence of the counterfeiting plant destroyed,

government agents would have nothing against him.

Kay had no choice. But a scheme suddenly came to her mind. She said:

"Do you know where Cara Noma's shop is?"

"No," the Chinese replied.

Kay did not believe him, but she said, "You will find it two blocks up from the waterfront, not far from the Chinese restaurant. Lotus Wong is living in an apartment above the shop."

Kay hoped that by this time the police were holding Cara Noma and guarding the shop. If Foochow went there, they would no doubt question him and trail him. Then he might be captured!

Without a word Foochow climbed the rail and went over the side of the ship. Kay watched him pull away in a rowboat.

The forty minutes were nearly up. What were Wendy, Betty and Lotus Wong doing? With the *Wingate* gone from the pier, what could they do?

"Oh, if I could only do something!" Kay thought desperately.

As best she could, Kay tried to estimate the distance to shore. It was a long swim, but she did not believe that it could possibly be more than half a mile. The water was calm and the current was in her favor.

Suddenly Kay made up her mind. She would try to swim it!

With a speed which astonished her captors, Kay climbed the railing and dived. She struck the water cleanly, and did not emerge to the surface until she was some distance from the *Wingate*. She could hear angry shouts from the deck, but the men made no attempt to come after her.

Kay's release gave her new energy. She struck out with powerful strokes which carried her along at a steady, even pace. It should not take her more than twenty minutes to reach shore, she figured, yet it seemed like hours before her feet touched the sandy bottom.

Foochow's rowboat was tied up, but the man was not in sight. On the pier, however, stood the Worth twins and Lotus Wong. As Kay pulled herself from the water and called to them, they cried out in astonishment.

"Kay! What happened?" Wendy exclaimed.

"I don't have time to explain," Kay said, panting. "Let's find a telephone quick!"

Betty said she had noticed a phone booth inside the pier. The girls raced to it, and Kay called the police. Gasping for breath, she said:

"This is Kay Tracey, the girl who stopped in this evening to tell you about Cara Noma."

"Oh, yes. We went there, and we're holding the woman. She had the green cameo all right. Took it from a cabinet, she said. That was a good bit of detective work, Miss Tracey."

"Listen," Kay went on hurriedly. "There's not a minute to lose. I've just found out there's a counterfeiting gang aboard the *Wingate*."

"What!" the sergeant shouted.

"It's anchored out in the harbor."

Kay explained what had happened, while the three girls looked at her in utter astonishment. She ended by saying:

"I told Mr. Foochow to go to Cara Noma's. I was hoping you would catch him."

"Sorry, miss," was the sergeant's reply. "None of our men stayed there, but I'll send a couple down to the pier at once. Maybe we can catch Foochow before he rows off."

"If the police don't get here in time," said Betty, as Kay hung up, "I'll tackle him singlehanded!"

"That won't be necessary," came a voice behind the girls.

They whirled to see a young Chinese man standing there.

"Chang!" cried Kay. "How did you get here?"

He smiled. "This will surprise you all, I know," he said, "but I am a government agent."

"And you've been working in my father's house?" Lotus Wong cried out.

"Yes," the butler admitted. "I was assigned to watch your father. Unfortunately, every Chinese in this country became a suspect when the government found out counterfeit money was being circulated from Chinese centers."

"But my father!" Lotus exclaimed. "He is not a counterfeiter!"

Chang said he had proved this. He would have to tell more of the story later. Right now he had a little job to attend to. In his investigating he had finally become suspicious of Foochow, but he had no idea the counterfeit press was on the *Wingate*.

"You get all the credit, Miss Tracey, for solving that part of the mystery," he said. "And now I must go and capture Foochow."

He dashed off to lie in wait for the man's return to the rowboat. After he had gone, the three girls helped Kay into some of their dry clothes. Then they raced off to watch the next part of the drama.

Presently they saw Foochow stalking angrily down the side of the pier. As he was about to descend the steps to his rowboat, Chang glided from his hiding place and tackled him. The struggle was brief, and the government agent won easily.

Foochow began declaring his innocence, but when Kay walked forward, he stopped speaking and looked as if some supernatural being had suddenly confronted him. His fright gone, he said he would admit everything.

He confirmed Chang's statement that Mr. Wong was not a member of the counterfeit gang. When Foochow learned that Lotus's father made exquisite jewel boxes, he ordered some for himself from time to time. They were to have a secret compartment in them.

The boxes were delivered to an oriental shop in Lincoln, which Foochow used as a front. Later Trexler would come there and take the boxes to his underground workshop to ship away.

"Trexler is stupid!" Foochow said. "It was easy for me to go there and slip the money into the boxes and leave the shipping addresses."

Chang was just about to leave with his prisoner when the local police arrived, and he turned the man over to them. A moment later they saw a police boat on the water heading toward the *Wingate*.

"They'll round that gang up in short order," one of the local men said.

Suddenly Lotus Wong hugged Kay. "You're shivering," she said. "Let's go to my apartment right now."

The girls drove to it, and Lotus insisted that Kay put on a complete set of dry clothes. Then she prepared a meal for them. As they sat around watching her, Lotus kept praising Kay over and over.

"You are the dearest friend in all the world," she said, smiling. "My parents and I will always be grateful to you."

Kay was embarrassed, saying that the excitement

she had had and the fun of having solved the mystery was enough reward for her.

It was not until two days later when Mr. and Mrs. Wong and Lotus gave a big party for Kay at their estate, inviting all her friends, that the full story came out. Seeing the Wongs' stolen furniture back in place, Kay asked how it had been returned.

"Mr. Trexler had it all the time," Mr. Wong revealed. "He will be in prison for a while. His business methods were always shady, but when he took to stealing, that was a real crime."

"What became of his fiancée?" Kay asked.

Mr. Wong said that the girl had disappeared. Although she knew Trexler was copying old pieces of furniture and selling them as valuable antiques, she, herself, was innocent, and no doubt glad she had not already married the thief.

"There's just one part of this mystery that's still a puzzle," said Kay. "What man reached through that secret panel and took the green cameo from me?"

"I'm guilty," admitted Mr. Wong. "I thought it would cure my wife of her fear about the cameo. Later I put it back in the cabinet."

Mrs. Wong smiled. "But Kay Tracey one who banish curse," she said. "Lily Wong never forget."

She and the girl detective exchanged understanding smiles.

"Father," said Lotus Wong presently, "may I present Kay with the gift we have for her?"

"Please do."

Lotus went to the cabinet and brought out a jewelry box exactly like her own.

"This is for you, Kay," she declared warmly. "It is from the Wongs to show our everlasting appreciation."

KAY TRACEY®
MYSTERIES

Kay Tracey—an amateur detective so sharp that even the best professional might envy her skills. You'll want to follow all these suspense-filled adventures of Kay and her friends.

By Frances K. Judd

15080	THE DOUBLE DISGUISE #1	$1.75
15081	IN THE SUNKEN GARDEN #2	$1.75
15082	THE SIX FINGERED GLOVE MYSTERY #3	$1.75
15070	THE MANSION OF SECRETS #4	$1.75
15071	THE GREEN CAMEO MYSTERY #5	$1.75
15072	THE MESSAGE IN THE SAND DUNES #6	$1.75

Buy them at your local bookstore or use this handy coupon for ordering: